Park Percy Nevill

Some Recollection in the Life of Lieut.-Colonel Nevill

Park Percy Nevill

Some Recollection in the Life of Lieut.-Colonel Nevill

ISBN/EAN: 9783337416409

Printed in Europe, USA, Canada, Australia, Japan

Cover: Foto ©Raphael Reischuk / pixelio.de

More available books at **www.hansebooks.com**

SOME RECOLLECTIONS

IN

THE LIFE

OF

Lieut.-Col. P. P. NEVILL,

LATE MAJOR 63rd REGIMENT.

COX & WYMAN,

LINCOLN'S INN STEAM PRINTING WORKS,

GREAT QUEEN STREET, LONDON, W.C.

1864.

TO

THE RIGHT HONOURABLE

THE EARL OF ABERGAVENNY,

ETC. ETC. ETC.

ERIDGE ;CASTLE.

PREFACE.

In compliance with the wishes of an only
Brother and some few of my old Comrades
who are yet alive, I venture to publish these
Recollections of my Life.

P. N.

1, Castle Yard, Windsor.
    December, 1863.

ERRATA.

Page   5, line 8, *for* Sabuzal *read* Sabugal.

,,   34, ,, 19, *for* Haste *read* Hoste.

,,   46, ,, 17, *for* Aubervillores *read* Aubervilliers.

,, 184, ,,   9, *for* polished marble *read* polished as marble.

,, 198, last line, *for* Peishwar, *read* Peishwa.

,, 42, 9 line, for Rear. read Front, Waterloo was

,, faught, about 9 miles in front, of Halle.

RECOLLECTIONS,

&c. .

CHAPTER I.

1794—1812.

IT happens that I am the son of a soldier, but not of a veteran one.

My father, who served in the old American War, used to amuse me, and raise my martial desires sometimes, by an account of his deeds of arms, particularly at the battle of Bunker's Hill, where it was said, he behaved very well.

He had a sword of a formidable kind, and being a powerful man, he used to whirl this weapon with much rapidity round his head, and show me how he slew two men who attacked him when leading on his platoon against the enemy.

Being on leave from the army, he met, at a *soirée* in Dublin Castle, the grand-daughter of his friend Lieut.-Colonel Pepper, of Ballygarth

B

Castle, county Meath. This lady, whom my
father induced to marry him, was my honoured
mother.

My father disposed of his commission at an
early age on being offered a civil situation in
Dublin, and finally established himself there,
where I was born.

My relatives in England had for the most
part been military men, and I was particularly
proud of a grand-uncle who served under King
George II., and who led a charge of cavalry at
the battle of Dettingen in 1743. Before this
charge took place, the king had ordered his
cavalry forward by *échelon* of squadrons from
the right, but from some mistake in the order,
they advanced to the front, without changing
the direction required.

Lieut.-General Nevill, who commanded the
cavalry, ordered the trumpets to sound the
charge, and he at their head, in his ardour
to attack, calling out " Dash along, my brave
men," pressed on, and nearly upset the king
and his staff.

Whether this anecdote be true or not, certain
it is that the general succeeded in his charge
against the enemy's centre, which circumstance
mainly caused our army to gain the day.

Having at college received a pretty good

military education, and a few prizes, I obtained
a commission in the 30th Regiment when sixteen years of age, and in a few weeks after
proceeded to the depôt of that regiment and
applied to join the 2nd Battalion, stationed at
Cadiz, during its siege in 1810 by Marshal
Soult. In the August of that year, the detachment to which I belonged arrived there, and
never shall I forget the striking effect this
beautiful city and harbour had upon us on our
approach to it, about five o'clock in the evening
of a fine day. There our fleet lay, and at that
hour each ship fired the signal gun, and in the
air at that moment were some large shells,
fired by the enemy, which were seen bursting
over the city and the fleet; but they appeared
to do little harm and were not much heeded in
the town, for around its sea-board were seen
crowds of Spanish women, some splendidly
dressed, who, with their cavaliers, were pro-
menading about, intermingled with British and
Spanish officers in full dress. There were also
numerous monks and friars in their varied
costumes, and altogether it was a novel and
impressive sight.

About the middle of September the battalion
was ordered to hold itself in readiness to embark for Lisbon. We got on board two days

after, and on the 30th arrived at that place, where an order awaited us to march to join the 5th Division of Lord Wellington's army, which we accordingly did, after the battle of Busaco had been fought and gained a short time before. In October, the army went into winter quarters, protected by the celebrated lines of Torres Vedras from the threatened attack of Marshal Massena's numerous army, the head-quarters of which were on our front, at the town of Santarem. The French army were cantoned in villages around that town, or occupied such quarters as they could get, in their own rear.

The army remained in the lines of Torres Vedras until the spring of 1811, and were occupied in strengthening those lines and in the usual exercise and drill of regiments. General Beresford, who commanded the Portuguese levies, took this favourable opportunity of getting them into a good state of discipline. In the meantime no serious attack on us took place, though there were some outpost fights, which were always repelled by our pickets.

The Marshal Prince of Essling, seeing little chance of success in forcing our strong position, and having lost a great number of his men by sickness and want of supplies, retreated through Portugal. His army was divided

into three great bodies, which relieved each
other alternately, in order to check our advance,
and under the guidance of Marshal Ney, in a
masterly manner reached the frontiers, crossed
the river Agueda, and established themselves in
a strong position there.   Ere this took place,
some brilliant affairs or combats occurred at
Pombal, Redhinia, Alfayates, and Sabuzal, &c.,
where the enemy exhibited much skill in de-
fending their retreating army; but they were
driven back at length, chiefly by the celebrated
Light Division of Lord Wellington's army.

When the enemy crossed the Agueda, they
appeared to leave the fortress of Almeida to its
fate, and our army occupied a strong position
on the banks of the same river opposite to the
enemy, investing Almeida with the 6th Division,
but not closely.   Here we remained some time
watching each other's army; at length, on the
3rd and 5th of May was fought the battle of
Fuentes d'Onoro, and gained by us.   Some time
after, the garrison of Almeida made a gallant
attempt to escape from this fortress, after
having destroyed the guns and mined the fortifications.   General Brenier, who commanded,
took advantage of a dark night, and having
formed his garrison in one close body, his baggage in the centre, escaped, being unobserved

by the pickets about the fortress,* to the bridge of Barba del Puerco, across the Agueda. Lord Wellington, who had some previous knowledge of this attempt to escape on the part of the garrison, had ordered a strong regiment of our brigade, the 2nd of the 5th Division, to occupy the bridge in question, supported by the light companies of the brigade. Unfortunately through the darkness of the night, the advancing regiment missed its way. The light companies who marched later reached the bridge about daylight, just as the rear of the garrison was passing, which they instantly attacked, capturing about two hundred and fifty men and some baggage: the rest escaped to the French army, who retreated, and immediately after appeared the missing regiment. The light company I belonged to, with the others engaged†, lost no time in opening French knapsacks and securing their valuable contents, and the officers had some trouble to get them into order, and secure the prisoners.

We visited Almeida, although from the frequent explosions round the works of the place, it was rather dangerous, but only two men

* Excepting the pickets of General Pack, who at once gave an alarm, but it was too late.

† The cavalry picket.

were injured. As we entered the town we saw the few remaining inhabitants outside their doors, looking in a most deplorable state, seemingly starving : some of us relieved the poor creatures as well as we could.

The much exhausted enemy retired into Spain to their supplies, leaving only some troops on the frontiers, and we were glad to have some rest. The commander of the forces was anxiously looking out for reinforcements from home, and doing anything and everything his great and fertile mind could possibly do, to get his army into good order. It appears from the account of eminent writers on this war, that Lord Wellington at this period, had no more than nineteen thousand *effective* English in the field, and something like ten thousand Portuguese, a force quite inadequate to attack the enemy.

In the north, the main body of the army continued to remain, for the most part of 1811, in their cantonments, without being attacked ; but in June, the French Marshal Marmont, an able tactician, advanced with his army to measure swords with Lord Wellington, who had received reinforcements, making up the English army to thirty thousand men, and a well-disciplined Portuguese force.

To the south, his lordship had detached two divisions of his army, with two divisions of Portuguese troops, and a brigade of cavalry,* to Marshal Beresford, who on their arrival immediately commenced laying siege to the strong fortress of Badajoz, situated near the south frontier of Portugal. Here he was joined by some ten thousand men of the Spanish army, but they were badly disciplined, and badly officered, and therefore not much to be depended on.

Marshal Beresford attacked fort St. Christoval, a strong work on the left bank of the Guadiana river, on a hill overlooking Badajoz ; here he had his principal battery, and made a breach, which he attempted to storm, but failed, when Marshal Soult advanced with a French army of twenty thousand men to raise the siege, and this brought on one of the most sanguinary battles on record. Marshal Beresford had hardly time to place his army in position to cover Badajoz, when he was attacked at Albuera by the enemy. The Marshal's strength in British troops was seven thousand five hundred men, with eight thousand disciplined

---

* At this time the 13th Dragoons made a brilliant charge on a large detachment of the enemy, in convoy of stores for Badajoz, which they captured, but were not supported.

Portuguese, and a large division of the Spanish army, though these latter appear to have done but little in the fight. The French fought with the utmost determination to gain the day, but so stoutly were they opposed, principally by the British troops, that they failed. The Fusilier brigade covered itself with glory in this action.

It is not for me, who was not there, and a very young officer, as I was then, to give a detailed description of this battle, or any other, neither do I think it possible for a regimental officer to do so; for when he is present with his regiment in a battle, he has quite enough to do to attend to his own immediate duty. Suffice it, therefore, for me to say, that out of the before mentioned seven thousand five hundred British, they lost in killed and wounded, most of the last severely, four thousand three hundred men. The Portuguese lost about four hundred, and the Spanish army somewhat more, in this battle of Albuera, which we gained, and Marshal Soult, having lost eight thousand men, retired.

Marshal Beresford then attempted to take fort St. Christoval, but failed. Lord Wellington hastened to the spot, raised the siege, and re- turned to the north with his whole army, excepting a strong division of troops placed under General Hill, to observe the south.

Marshal Marmont, having on the north frontier declined to meet Lord Wellington, retired
to his supplies at Salamanca. During the remainder of the year 1811 we remained in cantonments, excepting when threatened by the
enemy, either north or south, when we had
many a weary march to meet them, but nothing
of consequence took place.

In the beginning of January, 1812, Lord
Wellington assumed the offensive ; crossed the
Aguedawith his Light Division, stormed a strong
work on a sloping hill overlooking Ciudad Rodrigo, and supported by the 3rd Division and the
Portuguese troops, &c., under General Pack, laid
close siege to that fortress, which is on rising
ground on the right bank of the Agueda.   The
inner walls are of the old system of defence,
but a *fausse-braie* on the modern system of fortification surrounds it, resting on the river face,
and making it a place of much strength.

It was at this siege I became first employed
to act as an assistant-engineer, and was set to
work in making gabions and *fascines* for the
batteries. In a few days we carried a fortified
convent which annoyed us, and our parallels
were constructed with such good will, that in
a week we made an advanced breaching-battery
before the work on the hill, which we had

already captured, and mounted our guns, from which we battered in a breach. Here we had twenty-two 24-pounders and a smaller battery on the left to breach a flank work destined for the Light Division to storm. On the 19th both breaches were ready. The great breach in our front was immediately stormed and taken by the 3rd Division and General Pack; whilst the Light Division stormed the small breach on the left. Both were gallantly taken; but we unfortunately lost one of the best officers of our army—General Crawford, commanding the Light Division. General Mackinnon and several men were blown up by a mine on entering the great breach; but our loss, though heavy, was not so very great, considering the result.

Immediately on capturing the place, we set to work in repairing the breaches and strengthening the outwork first taken on the opposite hill. In the meantime the French army under Marmont advanced, but on finding the place had fallen, retired.

For this conquest Lord Wellington was made an earl, which we all were rejoiced to hear.

The breaches being repaired, the place was given over to the Spanish army, and the Earl of Wellington lost no time in marching to the south, where he crossed the Guadiana and laid siege to Badajoz. I found myself in orders to act as assistant-engineer, and attached to a brigade for that purpose.

We commenced our parallels on the 17th of March,* and continued them under torrents of rain, which deluged the trenches, the camp, and everything about us. This weather continued several days, and we were often above our knees in water; but our men worked with an ardour beyond all praise—the Royal Engineer officers and their assistants had only to tell them what to do, and it was done.

At length the weather became fine and warm, which soon enabled us to clear the trenches of water, and we were then able to get up some batteries to keep down the enemy's fire, which galled us very much, particularly from fort Piccurina and the ravelin of St. Roque. Both of those advanced works were stormed in very gallant style, which enabled us to advance our parallels, and at length to establish our breaching - batteries. We had the guns used at Ciudad Rodrigo and some others, and when all was ready opened fire on the bastion of La Trinadad and curtain of St. Maria, and on the breaches becoming practicable they were or-

* For an account of this celebrated siege, read Sir William Napier's work on the Peninsular War.

dered to be stormed on the night of the memorable 6th of April, 1812. The breach to the left was to be attacked by the Light Division ; that on the right by the 4th Division, and the 3rd Division, well known as under the distinguished Sir Thomas Picton, was to assault the castle. On the other side of Badajoz was posted the 5th Division, the 2nd Brigade of which, under Major-General Walker, was to escalade the bastion of St. Vincent, resting on the Guadiana. To this brigade I was posted.

At about 10 p.m. on the 6th, the Light and 4th Divisions advanced, crossing the Rivellas and an inundation in their front to their respective attacks, and reached the ditches in front of the breaches, which had been partly filled by the engineers with *fascines*, and partly by the rubbish from the breaches.

The two divisions crossed over and began to ascend in silence ; hardly a shot was fired at this most anxious moment, but in ascending both divisions met with obstacles of so very serious a nature, that it appeared impossible to surmount them.

Midway up the breaches were tiers upon tiers of heavy planks fixed firmly in the breaches, studded over with long spikes, and a few fireballs from the enemy exposed all to their view.

They cried "Vive l'Empereur," and poured down on the divisions such a storm of fire, accompanied by live shells and powder-barrels, that the loss in those divisions became perfectly appalling. Notwithstanding this terrible ordeal our men wavered not, but stood the slaughter. A few of the men got round the planks to the top of the breaches, and there found also firmly fixed, large beams of timber covered with sword blades.

The French behind them cheered again, as they shot down those few men, asking "Why do you not come into Badajoz."

Fortunately at this awful moment the 3rd Division after two failures, escaladed the castle, and established themselves there. About the same time the 2nd Brigade of the 5th Division, under General Walker, succeeded in escalading the bastion of St. Vincent, losing half their numbers, but they occupied the market-place in the interior of the town. The castle being taken, and our men being heard firing in the town, the French were apprised of our having entered it, when they became confused, broke up into parties, and left the breaches.

This enabled the remains of the two divisions to overcome all other obstacles and enter the town also, infuriated almost to madness by their losses; and alas! no tongue could tell the atrocities committed on that terrible night. I witnessed one on entering the town. I intended to join the 30th, my duty of engineer being over, when I met my servant coming from the arsenal, where he and others had conveyed our commanding officer, poor Lieut.-Col. Grey, who was mortally wounded. He had his haversack seemingly well filled with plunder. I asked him where the regiment was; he answered that he did not know, but that he would conduct me to the camp, as I appeared to him to be wounded, having some clotted blood on my face. I certainly was hit in the head, but in the excitement of the escalade did not mind it, neither did I feel a slight wound in my leg; but as I began to be rather weak I took his advice and he assisted me to the bastion we had escaladed.

In passing what appeared to be a religious house, I saw two soldiers dragging out an unfortunate nun, her clothes torn to pieces: in her agony she knelt and held up a cross. Remorse seized one of the soldiers, who appeared more sober than the other, and he swore she should not be further outraged; the other soldier drew back and shot his comrade dead. Immediately after, some Portuguese soldiers appeared; they ordered us to halt, and presented their muskets. I said to my servant, "Throw them some of your plunder;" he instantly took off his haversack and threw it amongst them, when several dollars and other silver rolled out, and they let us pass. Had he not done this I am sure those ruffians would have shot us, for the Portuguese troops, I heard, murdered every one they met.

We got safe to the bastion, and with much difficulty I got down a ladder more than half-way to the ditch, when I could hold on no longer and tumbled down the rest of the way into some mud and water, which seemed to revive me. My servant helped me out and carried me on his back to the camp, where I got a draught of water, and I shall ever recollect how delicious it was. I was then wrapped up in a blanket, placed on some straw, and fell asleep instantly.

I did not waken on the 7th until nearly mid-day, when I saw Assistant-Surgeon Evans at my side. He had some tea ready, but I felt so stiff I could not move. He washed my head, which a ball had grazed, and extracted a pellet or very small ball which had entered over the left ankle joint, but was not in so far that he could not see it.

The doctor's account was, that the Governor

of Badajoz, General Phillippon, having in the
night escaped across the *tête-de-pont* into fort
St. Christoval, had surrendered in the morning
to Lord Wellington, but that the plundering
in the town was still going on, and that
the loss on our side was very great. And certainly the governor's defence of Badajoz was
most ably and skilfully conducted, and he was
well backed up by his brave garrison.

When the details of our losses came out, it
appeared that more than seventy officers and
one thousand non-commissioned officers and
men were killed, and that three hundred officers
and near four thousand non-commissioned
officers and men were wounded; total, five
thousand tried soldiers—a great loss to the
army.

We remained in camp around Badajoz about
a week, and in three more I was enabled to join
my regiment.

The French marshals of the north and south
frontiers could not well make out how Lord
Wellington had taken two such strong fortresses, so well garrisoned and supplied, from
them in so short a time, and after making
sundry demonstrations to attack us, retired to
their magazines of provisions in Spain, without
effecting anything against our army.

c

Portugal at this time had been so completely
drained of food and forage by the French
armies, as had been also that part of Spain
contiguous to it, that they were compelled to
retire to the interior of Spain for their supplies, while our army was generally provided
for by convoys from our fleet, brought up from
the rear, and cattle bought when they could be
had at a heavy expense, and always paid for on
the spot.

The head-quarters of Lord Wellington on
the north frontier were for many months at
Fuentes Guinaldo, whence he issued his orders
for the benefit of his army; while Lieut.-Gen.
Hill held his place in the Allentejo or south,
and where his division executed a gallant *coup
de main* on the French forts at Almaraz, under
General Gerard, taking the forts and eighteen
hundred prisoners.

Thus matters rested until about June, when
Lord Wellington, having received considerable
reinforcements, advanced to the city of Salamanca, obliging the French to retire, and be-
sieging the forts established there by the enemy
for its defence. In the mean time Marshal
Marmont collected an army of from forty-five
to fifty thousand men and advanced to relieve
them, but the forts surrendered.

And then commenced a series of manœuvres on the part of the French marshal, to frustrate the endeavour of Lord Wellington to advance into Spain, and also to drive his great adversary back and retake Salamanca. These at length brought on the ever-glorious victory of Salamanca, which was fought on the 22nd of July, 1812, and in which we captured two eagles and between seven and eight thousand prisoners, and in which battle the gallant French marshal lost an arm. Here I beg to refer the reader, for a beautiful description of this far-famed achievement, to Napier's " History of the Peninsular War." The Prince Regent of England, justly proud of this victory, elevated our great commander to the rank of a marquis.

On the 23rd, we pursued the retreating enemy, and our advanced guard of German cavalry under Baron Bock came up with their rearguard, composed of cavalry and infantry, charged them in the most gallant manner, cut through them, and captured three battalions of infantry.

Nothing now appeared to dispute our advance

* Ten French generals and upwards of ten thousand officers and men were said to have been killed and wounded; which includes all losses previous to this battle.

on Madrid, which capital we entered on the 12th of August. Our appearance was hailed with joy and triumph by all ranks; thousands of the inhabitants, bearing flowers and laurel, came forth to welcome us. As my regiment was passing the principal street, in succession with others, some ladies, handsomely dressed, laid hold of our colours, to which they affixed laurel, and actually embraced the bearers of them with the greatest enthusiasm.

We remained in Madrid until the 1st of September, and on the morning of the 7th, the army passed the Douro and took possession of Valladolid, while the French army under General Clausel retired on our approach.

On the morning of the 19th the army entered the ancient city of Burgos, and the French army fell back to Briviesca, leaving a garrison of picked men, over two thousand strong, in the castle of that town, under General Dubieton, an engineer officer of much distinction.

The castle of Burgos is situated on a height above the town, and is extremely strong. On the height was placed a battery of twelve heavy cannon. It was nearly surrounded by three lines of field works, the lower line embracing a scarp wall at the base of the hill, very difficult of access. At intervals, between these

works were *flèches*, built of masonry, and armed
with cannon. The whole was admirably constructed for defence, and amply supplied with
stores, ammunition, and provisions.

The Marquis of Wellington was determined,
if possible, to capture this place with the means
he had, which were very scanty indeed, but
time on the present occasion was of so much
importance, that his lordship was compelled
to attack this formidable castle at once, and
accordingly he invested it.

The 1st and 6th Divisions were ordered to
attack the place, while the main body of the
army advanced to the front, to hold the enemy
in check. For the siege there were present
only five Royal Engineer officers, the chief of
whom was Colonel Burgoyne,* with a few
military artificers of the Engineer Corps, and
some assistant-engineers from the Line, amongst
whom I was numbered.

The artillery consisted of three 18-pounders,
and five 24-pounder howitzers of iron, and
those cannon not of the best order, having been
much used and knocked about, and the supply
of ammunition very deficient.

* Sir John Burgoyne states, in a few lines to me of a
recent date, how wretchedly we were then off in everything
necessary for a siege.

Here it ought to be observed, that Burgos in point of actual strength was not to be compared to a regular fortification. Still its field-works were so judiciously arranged for defence, that in the present crisis it answered all the purposes intended, and that was to impede the progress of the British general.

On the hill of St. Michael overlooking some of the works, was constructed a hornwork, which the 42nd Highlanders were directed to attack. They did so most gallantly, but remained fighting for more than an hour without success—when luckily, the Honourable Major Cox of the 79th, with his detachment, broke down the palisades shutting in the rear of the work, and it was thus entered. On being taken, it was found to contain six pieces of cannon and the remains of its garrison—some seventy men, out of a strong battalion. Our loss was upwards of four hundred, including Major Pierpoint, a very talented officer of the general staff, killed.

Colonel Burgoyne directed a lodgment to be made on the crest of the hill of St. Michael, to cover the captured hornwork and keep down, if possible, the enemy's heavy fire from the castle. The erection of this work he confided to me, with a working party of two hundred of the Grenadier Guards, and it was fortunate for us, that the enemy could not depress their guns sufficiently in the embrasures of the castle to strike us, or our loss must have been most serious.

We worked very hard all night, assisted much with spades and pick-axes found in the hornwork, and in the morning there appeared before us pretty good cover; but the ground was rocky, and the earth difficult to raise, and it was the hardest work we ever had. In the meantime, a detachment of the Guards and 79th Highlanders attempted to escalade the lower line, but failed with much loss, and their most gallant leader, Major Lawrie, killed.

As the fire from our cannon did not make much impression on the place, and were so much injured that some of them could not be used, it was determined to make our approaches by mining, and the engineers with their assistants had an arduous task to accomplish. The first attempt failed: but in the second mine we succeeded, and the 24th Regiment gallantly captured the lower line on the evening of the 4th of October.

During the night we formed our lodgment, notwithstanding the heavy fire kept up on us, and the live shells incessantly rolled down from

the glacis of the upper line.   Then the
enemy made a most determined sortie, upsetting our gabions and in part driving us back;
but we speedily rallied, and had a regular stand-
up fight, in some cases hand to hand.   I felt
suddenly paralyzed and became unconscious,
until a hand pulled me out of some rubbish:
it was a sergeant of the 79th.   A ball had struck
me on the left shoulder, passing out through
the blade-bone.

The kind sergeant carried me to my quarters,
refusing to take my watch as a present.   On
afterwards making inquiry, I learned he was
killed, together with his gallant commanding
officer, the Honourable Major Cox.

Thus ended my humble part in this siege.
Our losses up to this time must have been very
great.*   Of the Royal Engineers, one experi-
enced officer, Captain Williams, was killed;
Lieut.-Colonel Jones badly wounded, Lieutenant
Reid wounded, leaving *two*, Lieutenant Pitts and
Col. Burgoyne.   Of the assistants, one—Captain
Kenny, 9th Regiment—was killed; Lieutenant
du Maresque, 9th Regiment, severely wounded;
Lieutenant Stewart, 61st Regiment, half his face
shot off.   There were but *three* left for the siege.

* Two thousand men.

Colonel Burgoyne, one of the two alluded to as having hitherto escaped, was the wonder of us all; he seemed to bear a charmed life, for he was almost ever in the trenches, mines, or lodgments.* The pain in my shoulder was very great until suppuration took place, the anguish then became less, and being able to sleep, I gradually became better. My quarters were in a large house, rather too close to the castle, and had been used by the French as an hospital. They did not fire at it, except they perceived any one looking out on them from the back windows.

The progress of the siege was so interesting to me, that I remained here until our resources had utterly failed, and the French having collected a large army in our front, compelled Lord Wellington to raise the siege and retreat. Having had a few days' notice of this, and being just able to sit my horse, I left on the 16th of October, and got on the road to Salamanca, where our first supplies were.

My baggage, not much, was carried on a mule, with a piece of boiled pork, some biscuit, and a bottle of sour wine; this was all

---

* The greatly distinguished General Sir John Burgoyne, G.C.B., still serving his country.

I and my servant had to subsist on for many a weary day.

By the time I reached Valladolid I was quite done up, and with my poor servant, horse, and mule, nearly starved. Three days of complete rest somewhat restored me, and having laid in a supply of grain for my horse and mule, and of bread, eggs, and chocolate for myself and servant, proceeded on my way, as the English army in miserable plight, pursued by the French, were approaching; but I was exceedingly thankful that I was able to bear up against the fatigue I was obliged to undergo, and I got on to Salamanca without much suffering. Here I remained two days, and felt so much better that I continued my journey to the frontiers, crossed the Agueda, and got to our general hospital and supplies. Here my wound, which showed symptoms of inflammation, was attended to, and I soon became convalescent.

At intervals, a number of wounded officers and men arrived, who gave a very sad account of the retreat, and of the great losses we had sustained in the last days of November and the beginning of December. The weather had become so inclement, that the army suffered privations, apparently as bad as did the army

of the late Sir John Moore, in its retreat to
Corunna, in 1808.

At last the English army arrived, crossed
the frontiers, and entered into cantonments,
having lost five thousand, wounded or disabled
men. The French army also halted and went
into winter quarters. So ended the eventful
year of 1812.

CHAPTER II.

1813—1815.

THE armies on both sides had suffered so much, that neither appeared in the least inclined to carry on offensive operations, so that the spring of 1813 passed away in quiet. The whole of this time, the Marquis of Wellington was, as usual, indefatigable in his exertions to restore the discipline of his army, which the late disastrous retreat had greatly disorganized. In the meantime he fortunately received powerful reinforcements from England, with tents for the troops, which hitherto they had been entirely without; and many other equipages of war, so that now he was better able to open a campaign than on any former occasion. His lordship had been to Cadiz, where the Spanish Government were established, and was made by them Commander-in-Chief of the Spanish armies.

In the beginning of May all was ready for our advance into Spain, and my feelings were quite excited at the favourable chance now before us of success, particularly as my wound

was quite healed, there only remaining a stiff-
ness in the joint of the shoulder, which prevented me from using my left arm.

But alas! a letter came to say, that the
2nd Battalion of the 30th, my regiment, was
so very much reduced in numbers from former
losses and late privations, that it was determined to send it to England. I had therefore nothing for it but to accompany it on
the march through Portugal on the return
home.

Nothing particular occurred on our march to
Lisbon; we were by no means hurried, and were
glad to see that the inhabitants had for the
most part returned to their homes, and many
were busy rebuilding their towns, which had
been so recently ravaged and destroyed. The
terrible scenes of horror we had passed in our
advance were no longer visible, and the people
cheered us as we passed them, and blessed the
" Grande Lorde," as they usually called the
Marquis of Wellington.

On our arrival at Lisbon we heard of the
decisive victory at Vittoria, and we noticed
some of our men grumbling, not without some
reason, at not having shared in that battle, as
they then might have come in for a share of
the enormous quantity of property they had

heard was found in and about Vittoria and the battle-ground.

About the 1st of August we embarked for England, and in three weeks arrived there without accident.

After remaining a week at Portsmouth we marched for Southampton, where we received nearly four hundred men from different militia regiments, which made us again an effective battalion. Shortly after we embarked for the island of Jersey, which we reached early in September, and were quartered in Grouville Barracks, on the sea-shore,—wooden buildings, said to have been erected by the Russians in former days.

In this healthy place we remained until December, when quite suddenly came an order for our battalion and the 81st Regiment to hold ourselves in readiness to embark for a particular service. The ships to convey us soon arrived at the port of St. Helier from England, and without any delay we embarked from that port, and sailed for the coast of Holland with a fair wind.

It may be remembered that in the first week of January, 1814, there came on a frost of a most severe kind. This we encountered when off Dover, together with tempestuous weather from the north, contrary to where we were going, and we were obliged to anchor in the Downs for several days, and had not our anchors held we must have gone on shore. During this time the frost was so intense that we were always obliged to remain below, and the sailors suffered so much that they could hardly manage to guide the ships. The wind at last moderated and became somewhat in our favour, when we again sailed, but it was not until the beginning of February that we made Helvoetsluys.

The troops were landed from ice-boats and instantly marched off by detachments to Williamstadt, where accommodation was prepared for them. Here we remained about a week, and each officer and man was served out with a warm blanket and two pairs of woollen stockings, for we left Jersey in such haste that we had not time to supply ourselves with those very necessary articles in such weather, and on such a service.

The cold was terrible, and the ice-boats that brought us on shore had to be dragged by Dutch sailors over nearly five miles of frozen sea, and we greatly felt the severe chill and cold, so different from the fine climate of the Peninsula.

We marched to join the force of about six

thousand men, under General Sir Thomas
Graham,* in alliance with the Prince of Orange,
who had been restored to his dignity by the
Dutch troops, on the French retiring from the
country in consequence of the reverses of the
Emperor Napoleon. The enemy had left strong
garrisons in Antwerp, Bergen-op-Zoom, and
other places, and it was those we were destined
to attack.

The British general occupied the village of
Putten, near the town of Merxem, which was
then occupied by the French as an advanced
post. On the road to Antwerp, round different
parts of our village, the engineers were at work
to make the post somewhat defensible by means
of trees, here in abundance, which they cut
down and formed into temporary breastworks,
to prevent any sudden surprise of the enemy.
This mode of defence was obliged to be re-
sorted to, as the earth was frozen down several
feet, so hard, that it was found impossible to
make use of it.

Some days after we joined, the 78th Highlanders were directed to take Merxem,† which

* Afterwards Lord Lynedoch.
† Colonel Macleod, their leader, was severely wounded,
ten men killed, and two lieutenants and twenty-eight men
wounded.

they did in gallant style, driving the French
out and taking many prisoners.

This success gave us an opportunity to shell
Antwerp, which we did for many days, but
without much result, for our means were not
sufficient to follow it up, and we could not
obtain a fresh supply of ammunition in consequence of the roads being blocked up with ice
and snow. The enemy, however, withdrew a
strong post they held on the Scheldt, Fort
Frederick Hendric, which was occupied by a
regiment from our force, relieved daily by
another.

It happened in the beginning of March that
the 30th Battalion were on duty in this fort,
when the French from Antwerp warped one
of their ships of the line down with the tide,
and opened a vigorous cannonade on the fort,
elevating their guns and some mortars they
had on board, and dropping in many shot and
shell over the dyke before the place, causing us
a loss of our sergeant-major and five men killed,
and an officer and several men wounded. An
Artillery officer,* with only one 18-pounder and
one 13-inch mortar, struck the French ship
frequently, and, it afterwards appeared, killed

* Lieut. Parker, Royal Artillery.

D

and wounded some men by the bursting of a shell, and the ship returned to Antwerp.

The General wrote to Admiral Berkeley, informing him of this attack upon us by a ship of war, and he immediately sent us a squadron of armed boats from the mouth of the Scheldt, where his fleet lay, under the command of Captain Lord Nevill, of the *Boadicea* frigate; but the enemy made no more attacks upon us in this way.

Having been made a permanent assistant in the Royal Engineer department, I was attached to that service for future operations, and employed in front of Fort Frederick, directing a breastwork for howitzer fire, behind which was a furnace, constructed for heating shot, so that we should have given any ship that approached us a warm reception. Captain Sir George Haste, Royal Engineers, Lord Nevill and his two lieutenants, with myself, formed a mess in the fort, and were well supplied with provisions by the country people. The sailors received theirs from the fleet.

On the 8th of March, about seven in the morning, our attention was drawn by the firing of the front picket of the 81st, that regiment being on duty in the fort at the time. It was caused by some French skirmishers, who had advanced on ours, from a body of French troops marching towards us along the dyke. We all instantly turned out, and the 81st formed a column facing them, when the enemy halted and gave us a couple of rounds from a light gun; we returned the compliment by an 18-pounder, and they speedily retired. We had no casualties, and it appeared to be only a re-connoitring party of the enemy. On another occasion, some boats on the Scheldt, from Antwerp, approached us, when our tars instantly made for them in their boats; and, although the enemy seemed to make desperate exertions to escape, two were captured, wherein were some sailors and a few soldiers.

Up to this period matters remained without further operations of any kind, until the British general formed the design of surprising Bergen op Zoom, the strength of which place was well known. About the middle of March the severity of the weather ceased, and a thaw commenced. It was at this time that the General made the attempt, and with nearly two-thirds of his whole force, on a dark night, succeeded in escalading the walls without much opposition, the water at the time running over the ice in the ditches; and we took possession of seven bastions out of thirteen, and the water

port gate; but no effort appeared to be made
to establish a body of troops in the town,
which had been done on all former occasions
of our sieges in Spain. With the exception of
small parties of the enemy appearing and firing
upon us, we remained in possession of what
we had got, and expected the garrison would
surrender in the morning.

But we found it quite the contrary. In
many parts about the works, close to us, were
houses of the town; and as daylight appeared,
the enemy opened such a storm of fire upon us,
from loopholes and from the windows, that
half our officers, and a great number of our
men, fell in the course of a quarter of an hour.
Major-Generals Gore and Skerrett were killed,
and nearly all the commanding officers of regiments; and then great was the confusion, for
there appeared nobody to give orders as to
what was to be done. At this crisis no one
thought of turning the guns upon the houses
of the town. There they were, all loaded, and
their slow-matches in readiness. In a short
time large bodies of French troops opened fire
upon us, calling upon us to surrender, which
many of our men did, throwing down their
arms. All was lost; and some of us sprang
over the parapets, or through the embrasures,

into the ditches, now with several feet of water on the ice. Some escaped this way; others were shot down in the attempt; but I was fortunate, and got over with only a few bruises.

Thus ended this most daring attempt to take one of the strongest fortresses in Europe. Two thousand officers and men were taken prisoners, and the commanding general applied for and received from the Prince of Orange a division of Dutch troops to supply his losses; but from this time until April nothing more was done, and, as peace was proclaimed after the Duke's glorious victory at Toulouse, the prisoners taken in Bergen op Zoom were released, and subsequently joined us; and the French garrisons marched off with the honours of war to their own country.

Then Sir Thomas Graham, at the head of his forces, with the Prince of Orange, made their triumphal entry into Antwerp and Brussels, and were received by the people with enthusiasm. And certainly the inhabitants were always very kind to us. My regiment, with many others, were quartered in Antwerp for many months, and about an equal number of our force were in Brussels; both divisions of the army, the staff, &c., resting from their labours.

Brussels was particularly gay, constant dinner parties going on, and *soirées* and dancing every evening at the public rooms, and also at the houses of the nobility; and at these parties the Prince of Orange and his suite were nearly always to be seen.

Many noble English families began to arrive, and the blooming faces of the ladies, and their bright eyes, were most charming.

Thus passed the rest of the year of 1814. No more war's alarms awakened us from our dream of happiness. Europe was not yet in a settled state, and the French army was particularly dissatisfied at the new order of things; so it was thought prudent to keep the force here, in readiness for any outbreak that might occur. It was at this time that we had war with America, and twelve thousand men, and the best regiments of the Great Duke's splendid army, were sent there. Well might the Duke observe, at the breaking up of this fine army, that with it he could go anywhere, and achieve anything.

In February, 1815, some officers of the Royal Engineers were sent to the frontiers, in order to reconnoitre the positions on the banks of the Sambre and Meuse, take plans and sketches of those rivers, and make reports of the same to head-quarters. At this time the whole of the Netherlands was formed into one kingdom, under the Prince of Orange. Namur and Charleroi were the places the Engineer officers resided in, and on application I was appointed to join them there. We made short excursions into France, where we were generally well received, and passed our time very agreeably, occupied with our duties.

It began to be rumoured that the army in Belgium was soon to return home, when, in March, news came that astonished us not a little. It was, that the Emperor Napoleon had left Elba, and had returned to the Imperial throne of France; that he had arrived in Paris without firing a shot, and that Louis XVIII. had fled, and was on his way to England.

It was now war to the uttermost, and we began to repair the fortresses, not forgetting Namur and Charleroi. Those places were occupied by a Prussian corps in May, and other bodies of their troops daily arrived, resting on the frontiers.

We had patrols between us and head-quarters, from the 1st Hussars of the King's German Legion, almost daily, and were informed that all the disposable troops in England had been sent out, and with them our great chief, the

Duke of Wellington, to take command of the army.

All was quiet on the frontiers. Occasionally we heard that great preparations were going on in the interior of France to invade us, and that Napoleon was collecting his veterans for that purpose. The Duke of Wellington was collecting his army, consisting of British, Hanoverian, Brunswick, Belgian, and Dutch troops; but the fine regiments of his late army, still in America, were sadly missed by him.

The Prussians had gradually increased on the frontiers, and by the 10th of June most of their army, under Marshal Blucher, were cantoned around us.

About this time a despatch had arrived from the Duke's head-quarters to Major Hoste, our commanding officer, to say that the Duke expected the enemy would soon advance and attack the Prussian position at Charleroi, and directing us to remain in observation to the last moment.

Here I beg to remark, that some years after the remarkable events of those times had passed away, I heard that a rumour was in circulation that the Duke of Wellington, who had supped with the Duke of Richmond in Brussels on the evening of the 15th of June, was surprised by the advance of the French army. The absurdity of this report must be apparent. His Grace knew all that was going forward. After supper, in Brussels, he mounted his horse and departed to the advance of his army at Quatre Bras, and by early morning was there directing his troops to resist the serious attack of Marshal Ney.

On the 14th of June some French cavalry were seen reconnoitring the Prussian outposts, and on the 15th the Prussians were driven back, crossed the Sambre and Meuse, and occupied Charleroi in force. The French advanced, also crossed those rivers, and skirmished with the Prussians. About 11 A.M. the enemy came on in force, and drove back the Prussians through Charleroi. The Engineer officers were on some high ground, watching the advance of the enemy; they had sent their baggage to the rear on the 14th, and only retained their horses bridle in hand. Some French Chasseurs had got to our rear, and it was now quite time to be off. We were well mounted, and galloped past them within shot. They called upon us to halt, but we had something else to think of, so heeded them not. They then fired at us, but we were soon out of sight, along with a patrol of the

1st Hussars, K. G. Legion, who directed us to
a road to the extreme right of the British
army, on our way to Halle.

We rode on all day, stopping at a farmhouse
at nightfall. Here we got some bacon and
eggs, and forage for our horses. At early
dawn we were in saddle again, and soon
reached our destination, at Halle, to a few miles
in rear of which place the army had retreated
on the 17th of June, and where was fought, on
the 18th, the great battle of the war.

At Halle were our reserves of field equip-
ment, ammunition, heavy cannon for sieges,
and also a strong division of troops, consisting
of four British regiments and a large force of
Hanoverians, all under the command of Sir
Charles Colville. We quite distinctly heard
the cannon of the fight at Quatre Bras,
and of course were most anxious as to the
result.

Having received my billet, seen to my horse,
and arranged matters, I had now leisure to
think of my corps, the 2nd Battalion of the
30th Regiment, to which I was much attached.
We were like brothers, so friendly did we feel
towards each other, and much I wished to be
with them.

Nearly the whole night I was thinking of

this, and towards morning I determined to resign my appointment, and join them. Having settled this matter, I fell asleep, and did not awake until 11 A.M. of the 17th, and then waited on our brigade-major, Captain Oldfield, who dissuaded me from resigning, adding that we should have plenty to do by-and-by. Our chief, Colonel Carmichael Smyth, arrived in the evening, and told us all the news regarding the battle of Quatre Bras; and that the Duke, with his whole army, had retreated to his position in front of the village of Waterloo, where he would await and give the enemy battle.

The next day, the 18th, I duly gave over my reports, sketches, &c., to the brigade-major, and consigned my horse and baggage to the care of a friend, mounted a pony I had just bought, and proceeded alone to the field of battle.

As I had not the least idea where my regiment was, the thought occurred to me to make for the right of the army, and thence along its line until I fell in with my corps; but little did I think of the difficulty of doing this, amidst fire, smoke, death, and the confusion of so great a battle. I persevered, however; but it was not until late in the day that I got to the right of the army, and where I received no information.

As I struggled along as well as I could, amidst artillery, cavalry, and cannon-balls flying past me in abundance, I was determined to join any regiment I could. At this moment a cannon-shot struck my pony, knocking us both over, and killing him instantly.

I now made my way to the front line, where I fell in with the 95th Rifles (afterwards the Rifle Brigade). Here I met with a kind friend,* Captain Logan ; but every one here was too busy to mind anybody, until, during one of the lulls in the French cannonade, a large column of the Imperial Guard approached our front. We were ready for them ; and it was about this time that another column of the same Guard was seen approaching us on the left.

At this moment a strong regiment of ours advanced from the front and met this left column in the most undaunted manner, preserving a beautiful line, shoulder to shoulder— not firing a shot until close to them ; then, after one most effective volley, they charged and

* Many years after, the above gallant officer became colonel and Aide-de-Camp to the Queen, and was my commanding officer in the 63rd Regiment.

defeated the enemy. It was done by the glorious 52nd Regiment of Light Infantry; but where were their late gallant comrades of the Peninsular War, the 43rd Light Infantry? Alas! not here, but on their return from America.

The column coming on in front of our Guards and the 95th were charged by those regiments in the most gallant manner, and defeated; as were also other columns of the Imperial Guard which had attacked the right centre of our army.

It was now getting dark. The army had advanced to the French position, who had given way on all points; and there we rested for that night, as the Prussian army, which had at last appeared in great force, followed the retreating French during the night, not giving them a moment's rest. Late in the morning of the 19th we heard of the result of this great battle, and the army advanced towards France without opposition.

In due course I made out the 30th, my regiment; but, on joining them, what a wreck did I see!—the field officers all struck down, and Major Chambers killed. Of the captains, all were killed or wounded save one, who then commanded the regiment—Captain Howard;

in short, six officers were killed on the spot, sixteen officers wounded, and half the battalion *hors de combat*. The other regiments of the brigade they served in, which consisted of the 73rd, 33rd, and 69th Regiments, suffered at least a similar loss. This brigade was on the right-centre front in the battle, under Sir Colin Halket, who was severely wounded. I was informed that the brigade was frequently charged by the Cuirassiers of the Imperial Guard, and that some of their wounded horses and riders rolled headlong into the squares. This brigade highly distinguished itself.

On we went to Paris, and on the 28th and 29th expected another battle. The French army attacked the Prussians at Issy and Aubervillores, and drove them back. The Duke soon had his army in position; but the French retired into Paris, and afterwards behind the Loire. On the 3rd of July the army entered Paris, and some time afterwards the Emperor Napoleon surrendered himself to Sir Thomas Usher, captain of the *Undaunted* frigate. And thus permanently ended this long and great war, and Louis XVIII. was again placed upon his throne.

The 30th, with many other British regiments, were bivouacked in the Bois de Boulogne;

and as we had plenty of wood, we made some comfortable little huts, receiving our rations regularly, and paying for everything else we wanted. Not so the Prussians; for everything they had was paid by contributions on the country. Soon arrived a corps of Austrians and a division of Russians, including a body of Prince Platoff's Cossacks of the Don. The uniforms of those men, fine in themselves, were superb; their officers particularly, wearing in their four-cornered caps flowing black plumes.

In August there were in Paris two emperors and four kings, and the Duke of Wellington passed the army in review before them, followed by the Prussians—a most imposing sight. The allied sovereigns then begged the Duke to show them a representation of the events during the battle of Salamanca, which he did, Sir John Elly commanding the cavalry which in the real battle was led on so brilliantly by General Le Marchant, who was killed.

In this and other duties the army passed the year 1815, when an order from England arrived to form our contingent of 30,000 men out of the 1st battalions of regiments, and send the 2nd battalions home for reduction.

We marched from Paris to Calais in December, 1815; thence sailed to England, and shortly after were sent to Ireland. On visiting my father, in Dublin, such was the respect in which he was held there, that the Lord Mayor and Corporation presented me with the freedom of that city, in a handsome box. In the mean time the 2nd Battalion was dis- banded.

CHAPTER III.

1816—1831.

O N disbanding the 2nd Battalion of the 30th
Regiment, there was retained under Colonel
Hamilton a large detachment of officers and
men, most of them wearing a medal which
they had so gallantly won in the last extraordinary battle.*   These men were to proceed
to India, to join the 1st Battalion, in the
spring of 1817.   We landed at Madras, and
in June proceeded to the regiment, then
on the march to Hydrabad, in the Nizam's
dominions.   On arrival there, the left wing
was sent forward, to be employed in the siege
of Asseerghur, a strong fortress in possession
of the Mahrattas, then at war with us.   Previous to this siege, the battle of Maheidpoor
was fought and gained, in which I got leave
to join the commander-in-chief, Sir Thomas

* And here I may say that our glorious enemy of that
day, now happily our friends, showed us the road to resist
them, until the last man fell. Evening was closing when
the advance of our allies in force, 20,000 fresh men, decided the victory in our favour.

E

Hislop, as a volunteer. On joining the Light Company of the 30th, I was present with it and other troops, in the storm of the Pettah of Asseerghur, and at nightfall was intrusted with the command of the advanced picket of forty men. With it I repulsed, at 2 in the morning, a sortie of at least two hundred Arabs from the upper fort of Asseerghur, and was thanked on the spot by our brigadier.* But the praise I received from my gallant friend and brother officer Macready was the most gratifying.

This important fortress at length yielded to our attacks, but not before we lost our excellent brigadier, poor Colonel Frazer, of the 1st Royal Regiment, and between three and four hundred officers and men. Thus ended the great Mahratta war, in 1817. The left wing of my regiment returned to Hydrabad, where we unfortunately lost a great number of men by Asiatic cholera—a scourge at that time only recently known.

Hydrabad was then a very desirable station. We had a force of some four or five thousand men, to whom belonged a number of pleasing

---

* Through some mistake, the important post I defended was neglected. The Arabs took advantage of it, sallied out, and killed and wounded many officers and men.

women,* who, in their *soirées* to the officers of
the force, were engaging and kind to all.
Then, at the official Residency, we had pre-
siding the late Lord Metcalfe,—at that time
Sir Charles,—than whom a more hospitable,
worthy, and delightful person did not exist in
India.

At this station we passed a few happy years.
There was no war during the time of any consequence, save some outbreaks of marauders,
who prowled about the high roads between
Hydrabad and Nagpoor—the latter the principal town of the Mysore country, lately captured by us; and in consequence of the
mischief to trade occasioned by the plundering
parties above mentioned, detachments of native
troops — one of which, consisting of a hundred Irregular Horse, was entrusted to me—
were stationed about their haunts.

I had the good fortune to fall in with some
five hundred Bheels (or plunderers), loaded
with booty and stolen cattle from the neighbouring villages, when I instantly attacked
them. They for the most part fled, and we
captured nearly all the property, including the
cattle, which was afterwards restored to the
right owners; we also took twenty prisoners.

* Particularly Lady Rumbold.

Some of the robbers stood well, and caused us a loss of two horsemen killed, and some men and horses wounded. On my report of this affair being received at head quarters with the prisoners, I was thanked by Sir Charles Metcalfe, and, through him, by his Highness the Nizam.

I have little more to say during our stay in his dominions. Sporting parties we had frequently, and hog-hunting sometimes. On one occasion a formidable wild boar, after a hard run, attacked three of us—wounded one officer in the leg, and severely injured my horse ; but was at last killed between us. He was capital eating.

On being relieved by the 46th Regiment, we commenced our march to the Presidency of Madras in September, 1825, and encountered the monsoon on the fourth day's march. On the morning of the 27th, about 1 a.m., we had a terrific thunder-storm, accompanied by lightning and torrents of rain. Some arms were destroyed, and a few of the men slightly injured. My tent was wholly destroyed, together with all its contents, including my sword, which was melted. I happened to be fast asleep during the storm, but was rather rudely awakened by the shock, when I found myself on the ground, wholly uninjured. It was a most providential escape.*

The 30th Regiment arrived at Madras without further accident, and on their being ordered home, I exchanged into the 13th Light Dragoons, and joined them in India in 1826. In this fine and gallant regiment I was some years; but as I was recommended for promotion to infantry, I was allowed again to exchange into the 26th Cameronian Regiment, and proceeded to join them, stationed in the Upper Provinces of Bengal, when I was attacked with so severe an illness in April, 1831, that I was directed by a medical board to proceed to Europe without loss of time, to save life, as medicine taken in India was of little avail.

The British vessels having at this time all left Calcutta, I embarked on board a good French ship, where I was most kindly received by the officers. We sailed on the 6th, and what with the sea air and kind treatment I received, I rapidly recovered my strength. But it appeared fated that we should have a very long and disastrous voyage, which I will try to relate.

* Major Dalrymple, commanding the regiment, reported the matter to head-quarters.

The ship was called the *Bengalie*, under
Captain Feiulette. The passengers, beside myself, were a captain, formerly of the Imperial
Guard; the widow of a major in the Indian
service, going home sick; and a young officer
of the same service. The lady was accompanied by a very ugly pug dog, a huge tom cat,
and a cockatoo, which appeared on bad terms
with each other.

Before we arrived in the Bay of Bengal, we
were driven by a sudden squall upon a bank
near the centre of the Ganges, called the
St. Mary's, and it required all the skill of the
master pilot to get us off. In those times of
sailing vessels the navigation of the coast of
Calcutta was most difficult,* and required very
experienced men as pilots. The Government
had instituted a regular corps of them, with
different grades, according to their standing
and experience. On the 14th the Bay of
Bengal lay before us.

Having seen a good deal of India, I left it
with regret. To a man without much money,
and of an independent mind, it is, from the
liberal pay allowed, far to be preferred to
home service. To the sportsman and the

* The shifting sands in the Hoogley and off the coast
render sailing in those parts very dangerous.

man fond of Arab horses, it is everything to be
desired. The health, however, is sure to suffer
from a long 'residence, which certainly is a
drawback upon its advantages. To the 20th
we had cool, favourable weather. We amused
ourselves fishing; and on one occasion a large
flight of flying fish got up close to the ship,
from which I shot several, lowered a boat, and
picked up five. They are good eating. Those
poor fish have many enemies, not only in their
own element, but outside : when they fly, to
get out of the way of large fish from below,
they are pounced upon by the feathered tribes
from above, who follow shoals of large fish for
the purpose.

We had a serious row between the cat and
cockatoo, brought to a close by the former
springing at the latter, and striking him with
his claws through the cage; but he was soon
rescued, and not much hurt. The screams of
the widow for her pet were awful. I was not
sorry for the mishap to the cockatoo, as he was
now confined to his cage. Before this he was
often let out, and perched upon some of the
company. My head happened to be a great
favourite of his, nor could he be removed
without some difficulty. The Captain of Cuirassiers and I got on very well together : he

had seen a great deal of service under the great Napoleon, was a man of the world, and free of its prejudices. Whenever he appeared to pray, he pressed his Legion of Honour to his lips. The French certainly beat us in good humour and fun. We often had a dance, in which all joined. We sang and played occasionally, and passed our time very happily.

I used to perch myself in the main-top, for the purpose of either reading or contemplating the glorious beauties of a tropical sky, ever changing, and forming groups of varied scenery lovely to behold. Up to this period, the latter end of April, our time passed away well enough; but now a succession of calms and squalls, accompanied by torrents of rain, were of every-day occurrence, and rendered our voyage truly uncomfortable.

We at length got near the Line, and there were becalmed from the 6th of May to the 19th of June. The ship lay like a log on the water, the tropical sun, bearing down upon us, destroying the little comfort we had, and occasioning all to feel more or less ill. One terrible hot evening our notice was attracted by a dark mass rising very slowly under and about the ship, which rather alarmed us. It was the opinion of the captain and seamen that it was a mass of deep-sea marine matter, separated from below, in consequence of some disturbance there, and accelerated in coming up by the long calm and great heat. As it approached nearer, we could see many luminous bodies on it, and it was supposed that this appearance was caused by animal matter. The French Captain of Cuirassiers and I thought that firing the guns on board might cause some effect. We did so, and after some rounds had been fired, the whole mass gradually disappeared, to our great relief. It may not have been the firing that caused the object of our solicitude to sink, but certainly it began to do so after the first discharge.

That there are many marine substances at the bottom of the deep sea we all know, and there may be living creatures there that do not appear except upon some extraordinary occasion; for instance, the appearance at mid-day of what was supposed to be the sea serpent, as seen from the deck of the *Dædalus* sloop of war by Captain Macquay and several of his seamen, on their passage, I think, from America, the description of which was given by the captain in his report to the Admiralty.

As I said before, we all got on very well up to the continued calm and intense heat of the

equator; then some disagreement showed
itself: the widow was often in a rage at those
on board not being more civil to her very
troublesome favourites; the pug dog became
vicious and bit at people, and at last disappeared; and I have little doubt he was
picked up, overboard, by some lucky shark,
as there were many of those voracious brutes
ever about the ship—we caught one twelve feet
long, which, after lying bound on deck for more
than an hour, snapped at the hand of the man
who was cutting him up, lacerating it terribly.

The most disagreeable man among us was
the ensign. He was constantly talking about
what he did not understand, and ever drawing
comparisons on the fighting qualities of the
French and English, and always in favour of
the latter—a dangerous subject, which at last
led to a challenge from the Cuirassier officer.
The ensign did not seem to like fighting with
swords, so I got him to apologize for his
rudeness to the French officer. We all as
much as possible avoided him afterwards.

We sometimes caught dolphins. The beauty
of those fish in water is well known. The cook
on board was a capital hand, and made good
soup and stews from anything; therefore fresh
fish was always very acceptable. A fish stew

one day was brought to table, of which I ate. heartily : I afterwards heard it was the tail of a young shark.

On the 10th of July the weather at last changed, and, with a strong fair breeze, we continued our voyage, rejoicing, up to the 26th. Then came on a heavy gale, which lasted more or less for two days. The ship leaked a good deal, from the influence of the sun upon her sides, which caused all of us, when possible, to be at the pumps.

On the 29th the Mauritius was in sight, to our inexpressible delight, and a pilot-boat sailing towards us. The pilot at last got on board, the sea very high, and many dangerous reefs above and below water. We anchored in Port St. Maurice on the 20th, having three-and-a-half feet water in the hold. Here, then, we were sure to remain some time, repairing the ship ; and we had to look after our goods and chattels, somewhat knocked about during the gale. To the great grief of the poor widow, her irritable cat was found crushed to death behind a large sea-chest. I had always a dislike to this animal, from his nastiness in my cabin whenever he had an opportunity. The widow lady left us ; also the ensign, whose loss we were not sorry for. The lid had broken off one of the lady's trunks, exposing its valuable contents of wigs and love-locks sadly tumbled about. The French officer and I took up our, abode in the Hôtel de France. Any one who has experienced hardship can judge how thankful we were, and how comfortable we felt, in a good room and a nice dinner before us. I was determined to make a tour of this island and visit its many beauties, and called upon the governor, Sir C. Colville, an old friend, who invited me to his chateau at Redway, seven miles in the interior, to pass some days there.

The town of St. Maurice, and the country about it, are something like a small kingdom, or principality, in themselves, so handsome and prettily laid out is the town, built principally by the French, from whom we took it in 1810. In the back-ground, a few miles from it, the soil is covered with rich vegetation, and then appears mountain scenery running up quite in alpine beauty, which has a very pleasing effect upon the eye of the beholder. The inhabitants, for the most part French, or their descendants, are a very hospitable and pleasing people.

Set off on the 29th of July to the Governor's, where I received a hearty welcome from Lady Colville. We had a large dinner party, where wit and beauty reigned triumphant. Next day went off with a gay party to visit the waterfall of Pampelmoss. We soon got in sight of the fall, some one hundred and fifty feet in height, and fifty in breadth, descending from a high hill, from whence a stream sparkled until it reached the descent, where it fell, and disappeared in the woods below. It was a charming view. Two lieutenants of the *Undaunted* frigate (in the roads), Sir Peter Parker and the Hon. W. Keppel, joined our dinner party to-day, and invited all present to a grand ball on board on the 17th, which passed off with a great deal of dancing and music, and closed with a supper, at which good-nature and kindness prevailed, as it always does on board our men-of-war.

In my tour through the island I was well treated by the planters with whom I stopped. They principally grow sugar-cane. Their yield is most excellent and abundant, but the country is sometimes visited by violent hurricanes, which often destroy the crops. This island has evidently been produced by some eruption of nature, as also the neighbouring island of Bourbon, on which is a small crater, which sometimes emits smoke. The Government roads are very good, and the revenue yields a surplus after paying all interior expenses.

Painted partridges are in the island, and there
are still some wild hogs, brought here by the
first settlers, and a few deer on the hills.   On
returning to St. Maurice, I was in time for
the races on the Champ-de-Mars.   There were
some good runs, but the pony and donkey races
were more relished by the spectators, particularly from the mistakes and frolics of our
friend Neddy.

On the 16th August re-embarked on board
the French ship, which had repaired damages,
and proceeded to the island of Bourbon with a
few passengers for that place.   Amongst them
was a French lady, I think from the old
noblesse of Normandy; and a more beautiful
woman I never saw.   There was evidently
something the matter : she spoke only of her
meals and cabin arrangements, regarding nobody or anything else.

On the third day the island was in view;
it is about a hundred and ten miles from
Mauritius.   On the morrow anchored off it,
and landed our passengers.   Bourbon rises
high from the sea at all points, and in rough
weather it is difficult to land without getting a
thorough wetting.   It forms a sort of parabola
of rocks, in many parts seemingly inaccessible.
In the only open roadstead before you, in a

mountain gorge, is the principal town of
St. Denis.   There is, when the tide is in, a
heavy surf beating against the rocky shore.   It
is a French settlement, and the governor was
General Clausel, a distinguished officer under
Napoleon I.

The streets of St. Denis are well laid out,
and there is a beautiful botanical garden outside the town, growing most of the fruits of
Europe and of India.   In the town is a good
and cheap *table d'hôte*, and numerous shops,
where one can buy either Paris or Indian
goods.

As the captain of the ship intended to take
in provisions and vegetables here, at half the
charge he would have had to pay at our colony,
we were told that the vessel would not sail for
two days.   The French officer and I proposed
to examine the interior of the country.   Its
extent is larger than the Mauritius—that is,
some forty or fifty miles in diameter; but the
rocky nature of its coast, &c., renders some
parts destitute of cultivation.

We started on our excursion on the 19th,
and made ten miles, on good roads.   Good
shooting was found at partridges, flocks of
wild pigeons, and some guinea-fowl.   We saw
several hogs, of a small species, quite black,

and very wild. I shot some beautiful specimens of small parrots, or love-birds : they
are here in large flocks. We were well treated
at a planter's house, but much disturbed during
the night by cockroaches running over us.
We returned with a good bag of game, which
was very acceptable on board : these, with
fresh meat, and some fine rock cod, made us
a capital dinner.

We sailed on the morning of the 21st for
the African coast, and there passed close to us
a very suspicious, rakish-looking schooner, with
a large pivot gun at her bows, and some fine
but desperate-looking fellows peering at us,
We made her out to be the same vessel we had
seen off the Line, and heard at St. Denis that
it was supposed she was consort to the pirate
vessel of " De Soto," captured by one of our
cruisers last year, having previously taken the
passenger and merchant ship *The Morning Star*,
recently from Calcutta, and with passengers,
both male and female, on board; also some
few invalid soldiers, without arms. This ship
they sunk, with most of the crew, outraging
the women on board to a fearful extent, and
plundering the unfortunate vessel of all she
possessed. " De Soto " and his crew met their
deserved fate at Jamaica afterwards.

We had two passengers from St. Denis on board, for Europe,—one a very tall, one-eyed man, who ate enormously and said little; the other a very big-headed, good-natured, farmer-like man, who could talk from morning till night of nothing but cultivating sugar-canes. The tall man used to amuse himself catching the pretty Pintado birds, with hook and line; and as he dragged them in, used to laugh heartily at the screaming noise they made. These he used to cook and eat, himself, for breakfast, though they are of very rank, oily flavour; but nothing came amiss to him, provided he had but enough.

The wind generally was tolerably fair until the 24th of August. We were running down the African coast pretty well, and hoped our ill-luck had terminated; but, alas! no. We were between two and three hundred miles from the Cape of Good Hope, and a few fine days would have brought us in; but on the 11th September it blew a gale right in our teeth, and we had to take in every stitch of sail. This foul wind and weather continued almost unremittingly until the 20th; and had not the hull of the ship been good, we must have foundered. As it was, we lost our foremast; our mizenmast split in two pieces, from the top; bulwarks gone, boats gone; in fact, when we were boarded by the pilot off Simons Town, we were a mere wreck, with four feet of water in the hold.

The men behaved wonderfully well the whole time through this long-continued bad weather; nor was it until our wine, spirits, and provisions failed that they showed discontent: then, indeed, a serious *émeute** appeared likely to take place, the men thinking their officers were deceiving them. However, as has been often said, when things are at the worst they are sure to be better: the fair wind came at last, and in a most wretched plight we reached Simons Town, Cape of Good Hope.

As I have before said, those who have encountered hardships at sea in the sailing-vessels of other days can readily conceive what a " north-wester " is, of long continuance, off the African coast, particularly off Cape Le Guilles. There, in a gale, the rolling seas are a mile long; when down you go in the trough of the sea, which at times makes a sweep over the deck, carrying everything away, and

* I joined with the officers and well-disposed men. There was great insubordination, but it passed off so well, and all on board behaved so kind to me, that I do not wish to relate the particulars of it.

deluging the vessel with water. I was most thankful to Providence that I was enabled to work day and night with the men, in good health, and free from injury. All the officers and most of the crew were either knocked up with work and hardship, or were injured by the falling spars.

The very tall man I have mentioned was not seen for days, and we supposed he had been washed overboard; but no: he had managed to get below—how, it was not known, as latterly, in the gale, the hatches were battened down; but when we made the shore, he was found tied in his berth, with the remains of a barrel of pork, which he lived on, without cooking, for several days.

Our commodore, Sir C. Schomberg, in the *Maidstone* frigate, was here, and, as an old friend of my brother's, I called upon him and dined with him, relating our sad voyage. He said it was sad indeed, for many vessels were wrecked off the Cape, and many lives lost. He kindly offered some of his men to assist in repairing our vessel, which would detain us at least a month in the harbour.

On the 23rd September I started for Cape Town, and in Table Bay saw the wrecks of six ships, with some of the surviving men working

at them.   I do not think there can be a more
melancholy sight.   Next day, being Sunday,
attended Divine service in the cathedral, a fine
old building, erected by the Dutch.   The
stained glass was very beautiful.   There has
been latterly so much written about Table
Mountain, the vicinity, and the interior of
Africa, that it would be needless to give any
description of what I was enabled to visit
before my return to the ship.

On the 19th October I was summoned to the
vessel, now thoroughly repaired, thanks to the
assistance from the English sailors.   We embarked in fine weather and fair breeze, hoping
for good times.   Nor were we disappointed:
we had hardly an unfavourable day, and
dropped our anchor off James Town, St. Helena,
about three weeks after.

The French officer and I visited Napoleon's
tomb, and I never witnessed anything more
affecting than the outpouring grief of this
gallant officer : he knelt at the tomb, and wept.
There lay the remains of one of the greatest
(if not the greatest) men of ancient or modern
times, who raised himself from a humble
degree.

" Sic transit gloria mundi,"

I could not help repeating.   Yes, there was

the plain flat tombstone, unadorned but by
Nature's own simple grass and flowers surrounding it, with the great man's crystal spring
beneath, the willows then flourishing above
it; and here were two soldiers, enemies in
some great battles, but now friends, mourning
the fate of him who certainly would have won
all had it not been for the " unflinching en-
durance and fortitude of British soldiers."*
But I could not help thinking that it was
ungracious, to say the least of it, for us, the
triumphant, to punish by banishment our
great prostrate foe, who threw himself upon
our clemency. We should have had nothing
to do with it, and it appeared to me a blot
upon our fair fame.†

On the 22nd November we made the Western
Islands, and as it was exceedingly fine weather,
we waited for a boat from Angra, with fresh
fish and oranges—a very grateful supply. As
we sailed on towards the Bay of Biscay, we
began to feel the cold wintry weather of

* Such was said by the glorious emperor himself.

† A few years ago I met, in Paris, this gallant French
officer, and he assured me that the visit to Napoleon's tomb
by our gracious Queen Victoria did more to conciliate the
French army and people than any other act of kindness
towards them could have done.

Europe; and on entering the bay, on the 3rd of December, encountered a gale, but in our favour. It blew so hard, we were obliged to take in every bit of sail, and make for the Isle de Rhé, where we arrived on the 6th.

The weather now being fine, we dropped down the coast of France to Rochelle, which we reached without accident. And so ended our voyage from India, I think one of the longest ever known, excepting in the case of Columbus on his voyage of discovery for a new world. We parted from our messmates with regret, and we all interchanged presents of remembrance; and the captain, officers, and crew cheered me on entering a boat from the shore; my comrade, the brave French officer, displaying his Cross of Honour, saying how well I deserved to have it.

Next morning I started for Paris, and put up at the Hôtel du Jour, Rue du Jour, where I remained some days, very comfortable. Hearing that King Louis Philippe was to have a grand review, I attended, when thirty thousand men, cavalry, infantry, and artillery, passed before the king. They were well appointed, but not in the splendid way they used to be under the Empire; neither had the soldiers that proud bearing so marked in the time of Napoleon. The king was mounted on a superb English horse, but did not appear to ride well. I attended the levee afterwards, at the Tuileries, where about two thousand were assembled, amongst whom were a good many English officers, one of whom I recognized as having formerly served with him; and who, having seen in a French paper the account of our long passage and hardships, warmly congratulated me on being alive and well.

Having procured my passport, I left Paris, and arrived home in time to eat my Christmas dinner with my family, to whom I had the pleasure to relate all my adventures.

CHAPTER IV.

1832—1834.

MY sick-leave having expired, I applied for a passage to India, *viâ* New South Wales, having a great desire to see that colony. In due course I got a reply to say that if I was willing to take charge of the guard on board a convict-ship to Van Diemen's Land (now Tasmania), I should have it. In July, 1833, I repaired to Deptford with my guard of forty men and another officer from the depôt at Chatham, and embarked on board the *South-worth* convict-ship. The prisoners were put on board a few days after. On the 14th we sailed, and then the medical officer, Surgeon Evans, of the Royal Navy, attended by myself, inspected the prisoners. There were four hundred men and forty boys, all in good health. There were some fine-looking men amongst them, as also some terrible-looking fellows. There were three unfortunates, who had been gentlemen, and still bore the appearance of such: two were transported for forgery, the other for the manslaughter of his wife.

The ship had a formidable appearance. The bulwarks were raised as high as possible consistent with the navigation of the ship; across the quarter-deck was a barrier of oak a foot and a half thick; there were two embrazures, with sliding boards behind, at which were 12-pound carronades, ready loaded; twenty men and an officer were on duty, day and night; two sentries were on the poop, and two at the embrazures; the rest under orders there, ready for any emergency, with all guns loaded.* We fired off, in the morning, the loaded guns, when we all paraded, at 7 A.M. There were forty seamen, all experienced men-of-war's men, armed to the teeth, ready to assist the guard, or oppose any chance pirate that might appear. Two veteran quartermasters of the navy had charge of the seamen; so that we were well prepared for any eventuality. But the nature of this duty is so emergent, that it requires a man to sleep, as it were, with one eye open; and in a voyage of four months' duration becomes wearisome in the extreme.

The surgeon of the navy, beside attending the sick, was also warranted as a magistrate

* The prisoners were divided into four bodies, one of which was allowed to be on deck.

pro tem., and could punish by flogging, or reducing the food to bread and water, refractory convicts. He had an allowance of half a sovereign for every man he landed in the colony, besides other allowances; the guard had nothing but their passage paid for, and their rations, each a double allowance. Lieut. Chaproniere, of the 55th Regiment, was the other military officer, whom I knew at Chatham. He was an amusing fellow, fond of smoking and jollity. He generally got to the mizen-top, to be away from our barrel of cartridges, and there sing some amusing love ditties.

We cleared the Bay of Biscay on the 23rd, having good wind and weather, which happily continued until we neared the trade winds. Before this, there appeared off Teneriffe a fine rakish-looking vessel, that followed us for several hours, until evening fell. Had all the prisoners below, and hatches on, in case of any surprise from the stranger, until daylight next morning. We were all on the look-out, but nothing occurred. The captain made the same vessel out, but at a great distance from us. On getting to the Line we had only a few days of calm. Here some prisoners became ill from the heat. The doctor was very attentive to their health; wind-sails were employed to convey fresh air below. Two died of fever, one of whom confessed to the doctor that when a very young man he had murdered his father, a farmer, when they were at labour together, and then buried him in a small wood close by, as he was, which was never discovered, nor was he ever suspected, from there being no enmity between them that was known. He described the place of sepulture, and also a silver watch which his father had in his pocket at the time. What he was transported for was a highway robbery in after-years. The confession of the dying prisoner was sent home in due course, but I never heard more about it.

Fair wind and weather; the prisoners behaved well; few punishments took place, and these chiefly amongst the boys. We had them for the most part on deck. Some played draughts; others told stories of their adventures, or those of others; some few sung in unison together, and all conducted themselves decently, to our great satisfaction; so we got on very well indeed for two months, soldiers and seamen all healthy. Near midnight, however, of one day, we heard a terrible outcry from below. We were all as soon as possible on the *qui vive*. I, the doctor, some seamen, and soldiers, descended, and found three prisoners held down by some others. We learnt that they had contrived to get into the hold, and there were cutting away at a plank between the timbers, and had made considerable progress, so they must have been some nights about it, when some difference between them caused their voices to be heard, when they were discovered. They had determined to commit suicide in this way, by trying to sink the vessel with themselves: this was their account of the matter, and they said they had no enmity to any one in particular to cause them to do this. They had each, on coming on board, concealed a fine saw and a file, which were so neatly tied round with muslin that they escaped the doctor's detection when examining them. As may be imagined, we all became alarmed at this extraordinary discovery, which shows what a service of danger this was; for these men were amongst the quietest and best-behaved of any of the prisoners.

From this period nothing of any consequence occurred; our daily arduous duties went on as usual, and, favoured with a fair wind and fine weather, we got beyond our third month at sea. As we neared the south latitudes, whales were seen, and some days after a whale-ship came in sight, following several of these animals. The foremost, a very large one, we could see, as he came near, spouted both blood and water. He came at length alongside us, and actually scraped his huge body against the side of the ship. We felt a slight shock, but nothing more. Whether he did this accidentally, or in order to get rid of two lances sticking in his side, we could not make out; but we were glad he passed us. We could see he was evidently weakened by loss of blood. He was followed by eight or ten other whales; but, although they came close, they did not touch us. It was a curious and interesting sight, those monsters of the deep swimming about us, heedless of being seen. Two boats from the other ship now came up in pursuit of the wounded whale. The other ones either dived or moved away, but he appeared unable to escape; so they launched two other spears into him, and then lay to for the ship's approach, which we saw towards evening had secured the prize.

On the 19th November we saw land, and on the evening of that day passed Tasman's Head; on the 20th let go our anchor at Hobart Town. The breadth and depth of the harbour of the

Derwent River is here very fine; and the scenery, with Mount Wellington in the background, and the space nearly to its summit clothed with the graceful eucalypti and gigantic fern-tree, expanding and wavy, with many wild-looking flowering shrubs around, presented a prospect both new and charming.

To our great joy, the day after anchoring we were boarded by the two magistrates who were muster-masters of the convicts, to whom our doctor handed our prisoners over. They were landed all well, and for the most part received tickets-of-leave, in consequence of their good conduct during the voyage. The two men who tried to sink the ship with themselves, and two other refractory characters, were committed to prison. My guard was in very good order, and when we landed were met by the fine band of the 21st Fusiliers, who played during our march to their barracks, when we became attached to the regiment, and did duty with them during our stay here.

On calling on the Governor, Sir George Arthur, I met Doctor Evans, who introduced me, and his Excellency was pleased to compliment me on the care I took, not only as regarding the management of my guard, but in the assistance I rendered to the superintendent on board at all times during the voyage.

In my excursions around Hobart Town I could not but very much admire the ornamented cottages of the settlers, the owners of which, on settling, got a town grant at a moderate price, built thereon, and cultivated their gardens, which grew in abundance most of the fruits and vegetables of Europe. Fish from the Derwent was abundant; a small species of buffalo from the Cape produced excellent beef; and, in short, everything about showed the flourishing state of this country, with its excellent climate. The Derwent could conveniently hold hundreds of ships, trade was rising around, and the convicts had made beautiful roads to the interior; towns were springing up everywhere, and industry prevailed throughout.

A few months after my stay, I was offered, for a mere nominal sum, a grant of two thousand five hundred acres of land up the country, one of the few grants still remaining in the gift of the Governor; but I declined it, saying that I did not wish to leave the army and settle here. But little did I consider how valuable it would become in after-years; for such has been the prosperity of this place, that this piece of land would be worth at least ten thousand pounds in these days.

I agreed with Baron Hügel, the Austrian naturalist, to visit the interior, he to gather specimens of unknown plants, &c., I to have the pleasure of a talented and agreeable companion on my excursion. On we went, something like five or ten miles a day, putting up with settlers, or pitching our own small tent and living on our own provisions, carried by a couple of pack-horses, and attended by a ticket-of-leave man, whose conduct was excellent.

I had almost forgotten our trip to the top of Wellington Mountain. On our second day we were obliged to have a guide to direct us in our ascent, as the dense underwood and fallen trees would so much impede our progress. We had ascended about half a mile, when the fragrant odour from the wild flowers and flowering shrubs perfumed the air very agreeably, until we got to the top of the mountain, the ascent being about three miles. From the many fallen trees and tangled thickets we sometimes startled a snake, or laughing jackass, or a mocking-bird, that imitated the sounds of other birds.

We crossed over a bridge of eucalypti-trees

with some difficulty, as the foliage was so great as to impede the traveller, and under which we heard the roaring of a mountain torrent. After some time we were obliged to ford this stream, around which the fern-tree rose to fifty feet in height, and of so great a breadth that a company of soldiers could easily shelter themselves beneath it.

When we were within about a thousand feet of the top, the soil became scanty, and the rocks abundant. Numbers of parrots of a dark-blue, and bronze pigeons, flew about us, together with the wattle-bird, the head and neck of which were like our common cock. The cold became great, although this season of the year (6th February) was the advanced summer season in this climate. The last four hundred feet of our ascent was over large blocks of stone resembling granite, somewhere about twenty feet in diameter, well calculated for building material. These were for the most part nearly covered with a beautiful rich moss. We found it very difficult to get over the obstruction, but at length reached the top. There was not a cloud to be seen, and the view was sublime. We could see, as on a map, the whole of Storm Bay, the islands and mainland around, to the distance of forty to fifty miles, with the Derwent on our left, and the Huron River on our right, the banks of which were covered with fine timber trees. At this period this latter river was only partially explored.

We descended some hundred and fifty feet into the interior, and came upon an open piece of table-land, several miles in extent, sprinkled with low bush and other verdure, and the broom plant in flower. As we passed on, we shot some snipe of a very large size, also some bronze pigeons. There were some pretty winding rivulets, in which appeared sometimes a fish (herring size) rising at flies. Some of the mosses were in flower, red, blue, and light brown, of which the Baron, who seemed delighted with his prizes, as they were quite of a new species, gathered several specimens.

At noon we commenced our descent by the same way we came up, and when we arrived at our tent felt much fatigued in our limbs. We had been fortunate in our ascent, for, before the evening closed, a dense mist covered the whole mountain.

We shot, amongst other. things, a young kangaroo, of the small species. Its mother was with it, and another young one. They jumped up close to us, and on one being hit, the other disappeared, having leaped into its mother's purse or bag, in which it was born. This is a curious formation, under the outside of the animal, and a common one with other animals in the South.

We had just dined, when a furious wind came on with a whirling motion, upsetting our tent and eatables, and scattering them far and wide. These are of frequent occurrence in the summer months, raising clouds of dust; but they are soon over. Next day proceeded on our tour, and passing New Norfolk, fell in with a branch of the Derwent, and enjoyed some hours' good fishing. The fish before mentioned, a kind of smelt, was extremely good eating. The trumpeter fish, also good, is rather large and flat, and makes a blowing, shrill noise on raising itself above water, whence it is called by its odd name. As we neared Launceston, several very pretty cottages appeared, the holders of which, having various grants of from one to five hundred acres, appeared to get on extremely well. There they felt independent and happy; fine children rose around them, the parents sure of provision in their old age; cattle, sheep in abundance, with their splendid silky fleece; barn-door fowl innumerable, and plenty of wood firing, made them feel to want nothing. The young people used to meet at each other's dwellings occasionally—dance, sing, and otherwise amuse themselves more than half the night; then up, after a few hours' rest, to their different labours, either in the farm-yard or field cultivation. Had I not had such regard for my profession, I would certainly have remained, and, with a kind helpmate, enjoyed the pleasant, quiet, and independent habits of a settler's life here pourtrayed.

As we expressed a wish to see a kangaroo hunt, of the large boomer species, the Baron, myself, and others, repaired to a large tract of uncultivated ground, with the high brush-wood in plenty on it. In this is found the animal. We had several dogs, and an old friend had lent me his English greyhound, which accompanied me after considerable labour. We came on a male and female boomer, which the dogs roused up. They parted different ways, and my dog pursued the largest. The animal went on, making springs, some of them twenty feet in length. As everybody knows, they have immense, long, powerful hind-legs, armed with long, hard claws; with these they defend themselves against dogs or men, when they come to bay. Before this came about, the animal kept our horses at speed for a couple of miles; it then became exhausted, and sat up with its back against a tree. My greyhound fearlessly rushed in to seize it, but in doing so received such a blow as knocked him over; and before we and the dogs closed on the kangaroo, he repeated the blow, and with his claws laid the poor greyhound open, so that his death was almost immediate. The other dogs and men now attacked the brute, which made but little further resistance before he was killed. He measured more than five feet in length, not including his powerful hind-legs or short tail.

The birds we saw on our excursion were numerous. Wild ducks, the emu, the eagle, the black swan, and geese, were at that time plentiful enough; since then, few are to be seen.

As we had received letters at Launceston, stating that a ship with troops was soon to sail for Sydney, New South Wales, I was constrained to retrace my steps, and arrived in eight days at Hobart Town. I left this island of beauty early in April, 1834, in charge of my detachment and other troops. In the course of a week we arrived at Sydney in safety, and

I could not help feeling surprise at seeing this truly noble place—everything so English and fresh ; the London cries, and hawkers going about the fine streets to sell their goods, as it used to be in times past in England.

CHAPTER V.

1834.

I ENGAGED a passage to Madras in the *Edinburgh Castle*, Captain Barber, who told me that he intended to go through the inner passage, that is, through Torres Straits, which I was glad to hear, as there were many things quite new to be seen. Having given over my detachment to the authorities, I was preparing to embark, when I learnt that an accident had happened to the ship, which was of so serious a nature that it would probably detain her in harbour for some weeks. This enabled me to visit the country.

In Paramatta I met with an old brother officer of the 13th Dragoons, who was here breeding draught horses for the Indian artillery. He begged that I would take charge of thirty-two horses, he being in treaty with the captain of the *Edinburgh Castle* to convey them on board that ship to India. I consented, though I knew they would be a trouble to look after them.

From Paramatta I went to other places, where I was well received, and where I was nearly lost in the bush. Having missed my way while shooting, not a soul to be seen, nor a house near for miles, I bethought me of the miserable fate of Major Hovenden, who lost himself in the far wilds of this country, a few years previously, and whose remains were found, months after he disappeared, by the dogs of some sportsmen. Fortunately I had a very small compass-ornament to my watch-chain, in good order, and knowing the bearings of Sydney, I made my way in that direction with great difficulty, when, towards evening, I met with a road which I followed, and at about 10 o'clock P.M. reached a settler's house. I had gone many miles astray, and, had it not been for the compass, perhaps might have met with the miserable fate of poor Hovenden.

On arriving at Sydney, I met with an old naval friend, on his way to pay a short visit to New Zealand, and then return. I begged to go with him, which he agreed to. We had a short and agreeable passage. This is, if possible, a finer country than Australia, and the natives, in appearance, manners, and intellect, are quite a superior race. They come up to you with a confidence and bold bearing unknown to the natives of Australia, who are well known to be a miserable race. Both

Captain Stanley and I agreed in thinking they would give us plenty to do in governing them, and so it has turned out of late years.

On returning from New Zealand, I found that the *Edinburgh Castle* was ready, and the horses were being embarked. On the 12th of May I went on board, and the horses were given over to me by Captain Collins, with four farriers to attend them, and we sailed next day from the superb harbour of Sydney.

On looking over the horses, I found them more fitted for draught than the Arabs and country-bred horses of India. They were mostly from the Cape of Good Hope, and ranged from fifteen to sixteen hands high, full of bone and muscle, and were descended from horses of English breed. On the 16th we passed Indian Head, a dangerous reef, ten to fourteen miles long, which we were right glad to leave behind.

In a few days we made Torres Straits. The water here is so clear, that one can see twenty, sometimes thirty feet down, the coral rocks generally appearing white, sometimes brown, according to their age. It is marvellous how those minute animalculæ can form such masses, but so constantly are they at work, that in the course of time this channel will not be navigable. As it is—or was then—the captain was obliged to anchor the ship every evening, which gave me an opportunity of visiting some of the beautiful but small islands we constantly met with on our passage. They are mostly uninhabited, but are visited occasionally by the natives of a large group called the Murray Islands, either for the purpose of fishing or plunder. These islanders appear to eat everything they can catch, including human beings with whom they may happen to be at war.

After some days, the group of the Northumberland Islands were in sight. These are bold and precipitous, the cliffs covered with several kinds of sea-birds. I landed at the largest of them with one of the farriers. This man, in his anxiety to catch an animal resembling the land-crab of the West Indies, but four times the size, having thrust his hand into the hole which it entered, had it seized by the animal, and was unable to withdraw it without assistance. The bite was severe, though not venomous; but he was unable to use his hand for a week afterwards. Here I shot some beautiful green pigeons, with red bills and feet.

A day or two after, we anchored off the Percy Islands, which are five in number, and covered with verdure. The centre one is about four miles in circuit. Its appearance is lovely, having an open, white, sandy bay on one side, which glittered in the sun. An eminence, covered with grass and blue flowers, and from which descended a rivulet, on whose banks were groups of a species of laurustine, intermingled with the fern-tree, rose to the top of the island. Never could one behold a scene more tranquil and soothing to the mind, inducing one to feel a little poetical. So, indeed, I felt. I ventured to express my feelings in words, and here is the result :—

> " I know a dear, a lovely spot,—
> A scene of sunshine and of flowers ;
> And gladly would I fix my lot
> Amidst its smiling lawns and bowers.
> There sweet waters softly play,
> Telling to blossom'd banks their tale ;
> And Music's note and Pleasure's lay
> Glide gaily through that joyous vale.
> Yet think not that in bowers and brooks
> The best and dearest charm is found:—
> Oh, no ! 'Tis the home of one whose looks
> Shed light, and hope, and spring around.
> And, were it changed to trackless sand,
> Love's magic wand the scene would hail;
> And flowers and fruits of fairy-land
> Would flourish in the desert vale."*

---

* Pray be very civil, Reader !

I have no doubt that in later years the
numerous fertile islands of this strait will be
colonized. The only drawback is, its being
land-locked on each side, and the ever-growing
coral rocks. Passing on, with the trade-wind
blowing from the S.E., we passed Cumberland
Islands, two of which are eight to ten miles
round. On we came to Sunday Islands, two
of which are about twenty miles round, of an
oblong shape, and presenting a chalky appearance, with some scrub bushes here and there
upon them. Several fish, of a bright red
colour, one to two feet long, rose to the
surface and bounced about, seemingly in play
with each other, but they would not take a
bait. I shot one, but did not succeed in
getting it. Several of the other fish followed
it to the bottom, thirty feet down, where we
could clearly see them devouring the dead
one.

On the 31st May sailed past Palm Islands,
one large, the other small and rocky; then
on to Fitzroy Island, where, on the 12th June,
we took in a supply of excellent water for the
horses. Latitude here, 16° 55′ 21″ S.; longi-
tude, 145° 36′ 21″ E. This island was so very
pretty, and the water so good, that two passenger ladies (Mrs. Conolly and her amiable

sister) wished to land and roam about, and
to have a pic-nic on shore. The two ladies
and four gentlemen did so, and it was a
charming spot: the laurustine, a species of
laurel, with a perfume somewhat similar; the
mimosa and eucalypti, and various flowering
shrubs of white and blue, were scattered over
the velvety grass. We wandered about this
sweet place, and nothing noxious crossed our
path. We met with some long spider-webs,
and saw very large mottled-white spiders
running on them in quest of the many insects
and large moths which occasionally flew about.
There were cockatoos of a large kind, richly
tufted on the head; pigeons, green and white,
the latter with red feathers about their head.
Several were shot, and were good eating.
This island, about twelve miles long and six
broad, only wants the hands of man to make
it most productive, as the soil appears so rich
that it would grow anything, particularly tropical fruits and flowers.* We came on some
small fishing-huts used by the natives of the

* In some of the islands we observed, hanging from trees
near the shore, gigantic bats, or rather flying foxes. I shot
one. The wings, extended, were 2 feet; the body the size
of a small rabbit. They feed on anything they can get, and
are like a fox.

mainland, in their excursions for fish and a species of oyster which abounds in some places.

On the 20th we came to the Murray Islands, a group extending along the channel for many miles. Here we saw red and white coral-rocks rising several hundred feet, presenting, from their grotesque appearance, a most magical effect, from the sun glittering upon them. On these rocks were perched some natives—men, women, and children, totally nude. They were the ugliest people I ever saw, and are cannibals. I landed, and Captain Barber cautioned me not to go far from the landing-place; for, he said, " as you are still rather young, not bad looking, and pretty fresh, the natives, could they catch you, would have quite a treat in feasting on you, after you were nicely roasted. The ladies are said to prefer white flesh, to the cost of some of our poor sailors, who are known to have been eaten by them after being pounced upon when wandering carelessly in the interior." I therefore did not go far from the coast, and, having my choice double-barreled Manton with me, was careful not to discharge both barrels. It was well I did not; for, on putting up some sea-snipe, I knocked over one, and pursued the rest to a swampy cover farther than I intended. I succeeded in killing several of those birds, and, as it was getting towards evening, turned down to the beach, but was obliged to pass through some thick cover on my way, when, lo! I found myself nearly surrounded by woolly heads; and, before I could load the discharged barrel, I had four of those wretches nearly upon me with their clubs. With the loaded barrel I gave the charge amongst them, when they yelled and vanished. Not being aware of a two-shotted gun, those savages supposed I had the power to load it by magic.

On returning to the ship, I felt a little ashamed to tell my story, as the leer on the captain's face plainly told me he had already learned it of the boat's crew. However, there I was, body and bones, neither killed nor eaten, to the great disappointment, I suppose, of the black ladies. We picked up one of their canoes on shore, and so light was it, that one man might carry it. It was made with considerable skill, of palmyra leaves, curiously sewn together by the stringy bark of the same tree.

Up to the 26th we sailed on, dropping anchor every evening, until we made Hope Island. Here the coral rocks under water rose so near the surface that we were in some dread lest

the vessel would ground even at high tide, and
then the horses would be sacrificed by their
having to be thrown overboard to lighten the
ship. The vessel did, indeed, ground, but it
was at low water, which saved the horses, but
not, however, without much difficulty, for the
captain said, better to lose the horses than
lose the ship. There could be no doubt of
that. There was a slight wind in our favour,
but the probability was, that with the rising
tide we should get off the reef. The captain
was somewhat alarmed, and insisted upon
making sure by throwing the horses overboard.
His first officer and some others did not agree
with him on the necessity of the case, so this
gave me an opportunity of speaking. I said
my life was as dear to me as that of any on
board; but, as I had heard there was no real
danger, and it was nearly calm, I thought we
had better wait to see what would occur on the
rising tide. The captain said, " Well, I do not
think, Captain Nevill, you are so good a judge,
as you have so recently risked your life for a few
wild birds." I did not either like this rather
unkind remark, nor to reply to it; but, as I was
well backed up, I resolved to wait the result,
and resist destroying the poor horses. The
captain, prudently, I think, gave way.

In a few hours the tide rose under the ship so
high that, aided by the boats, we slid off the coral
rocks, and saved the horses and our heavy baggage.   The captain looked nearly as silly as I did
on my escape from the inhabitants of the Murray
Islands, and we were never cordial afterwards,
nor, indeed, particularly intimate at any time,
for he was always grumbling at his folly, as he
called it, in taking the horses on board,
although, as he acknowledged, the being well
paid for them made the risk lighter; but, as he
said, how would he answer to his owners in
case of any disaster?   That was his own look-
out; and if he thought it so dangerous, why did
he run so great a risk?   Indeed, the horses
gave us a deal of trouble, for they required so
much looking after, and many were rather un-
ruly tempered, as are some other animals. We
had only two violent brutes, who were always
trying to attack the farriers when clearing out
the stable, and kicking at the barricade separating them from the rest; they got up a row
amongst the others, and kept the farriers, with
myself, very much on the alert.

On the 29th we made Endeavour River,
passing several islands. This was a very
dangerous locality, and we were always on the
look-out, and the lead going. The sea was

H

very clear, but deceptive in appearance; and it was here that the celebrated first navigator of those seas, Captain Cook, experienced many difficulties, and where his ship grounded and lay for twenty-three hours.

Made Turtle Reef, which is so called from the presence here of those animals. We caught one—a timely supply. Going cautiously on, we anchored at Eagle Island, where a few of us landed, and picked up some enormous shells. Here, and on other islands, we shot several birds; amongst them a kind of curlew, black, with blue and white wings, and long red bill and tail. The others were of the duck, seagull, and petrel tribe. We continued passing several islands, mostly of the same description as those already named, but not appearing either so pretty or fertile. It was now getting very hot as we neared the Equator.

As we passed Bird Island we saw it covered with pelicans, boobies, a kind of goose, and immense flocks of sandpipers, and others too numerous to make out, and a kind of small penguin occupying the shore.

In 10° 36′ 0″ S. and 141° 52′ 50″ E. we met with the *Dryad*. She had encountered terrible weather before entering the straits on her passage from India to Sydney, and had lost her foremast, besides losing several of her men washed overboard. We gave them some supplies, of which they were much in want. They mentioned having seen a large vessel high and dry on a coral reef near the mainland, with masts and yards gone, and filled with natives, who appeared in full possession of her.

On the 2nd of July we gained the open sea, and had no more anchoring. Neared the very large island of Timour, famous for its breed of ponies. It is partly occupied by the Dutch and Portuguese, who possess opposite sides of the island, and have each a certain portion of territory separate. This island is more than three hundred miles round. It is extremely fertile, possessing, like India, sugar, cotton, indigo, &c. We landed at Copang, and visited the Dutch governor, who was extremely civil. Here our captain was to remain some days, taking in supplies and freight for the Indian market. Several of us dined with the governor. He had many Dutch gentlemen and ladies, who spoke English, and were jolly, good-humoured people, liking the English much. We talked a good deal about England and Holland, the Dutch people saying, " We are much alike, and never again shall we be unfriendly towards each other." A very stout, fair widow sat next to me during dinner, and I had the good fortune to gain her good opinions. She asked me to her villa, some ten miles off, and said the longer I could remain the better. This was most pleasing to me, as I wished much to see something of the interior of this thriving place. After dinner we had coffee, schnaps, pineapple wine, and such cool cocoanut-water that it was quite a treat. Later in the evening we had quite a reception of young people. The fiddle, dulcimer, and a fine old harpsichord, were not wanting; and the young ladies danced country dances and some quadrilles until morning. People here appear to lead a very happy life.

The town contained at that time about eight thousand inhabitants, and the usual cleanliness and regularity prevailed here as in Holland. The day after, I set off for the widow's villa, on a horse provided for me by her, she accompanying me on another horse. Our ride was delightful. The roads were very good, the cultivation magnificent, and numerous birds of brilliant plumage occasionally passed from one plantation to another across our path; many flowers also, from Dutchland, were there. The chrysanthemum, now so plentiful in England, was then an exotic but little known, but flourished here in abundance and in great beauty. We at length came to the lady's hospitable château, for it partook of this style of architecture, as well as the old Flemish very comfortable farmyard style. We passed from the entrance gateway through a passage to the interior of the dwelling, and from open apertures in this passage we could see several horses feeding, their stables being situated behind, which is a very good way of seeing the horses taken care of, without going round to the stables. The lady kindly conducted me over her gardens—handsome, and abounding in pineapples and fruit-trees. The banana and plantain flourished beside each other; the cypress and myrtle were abundant; and a cocoanut-tree here and there put me in mind of the refreshing draught I had from that delicious nut, the evening before, in Copang. Some days passed away in a most agreeable manner : some of the neighbouring families were asked to make up an evening party, and their hearty goodnature made everything agreeable. There were some very pretty young vrows, just coming into girlhood, without that stoutness generally attending the elder girls or their mammas; and their pretty, artless manner made them very interesting. There is nothing like roughing it a little; then

meeting with comfort and agreeable people
makes the enjoyment one feels ten times more
pleasing than otherwise.   Days slipped away
so agreeably that I thought not of ships or
horses, until a horseman handed me a letter
to say the captain was only waiting for me
before he sailed.   So at peep of day I started
for Copang.   Before I did so, the kind widow
put a letter into my hand, which was as follows:—" Why do you leave us ?   You appear
very happy here, and we—especially myself—
feel very reluctant to part from you.   I have
heard much of your services and travels, which
have highly interested me in your favour.
Stay, then, and settle down here ; and if I can
conduce to your happiness, I will.   You have
seen my pretty place ; I am independent and
rich.   But perhaps you have a favourite
looking out for your return home; if so,
it would be far from my wish to detain you
here.   So, pray, before you leave, write me
a few lines, and accept the enclosed " (this was
a handsome gold ring).   I could not but feel
highly grateful to this good creature for her
partiality, benevolence, and most kind feeling.
I wrote her a note, expressing how grateful
I felt, and assuring her that I would ever
remember and appreciate her kindness; and

begged her to accept a ring of mine, in return for hers.

Before leaving this interesting place, I learned that, prior to its being colonized by Europeans, it was so much infested by boa-constrictors of an enormous size, that the aboriginal inhabitants were deterred from entering the dense forests, for fear of being seized and •swallowed by them. When in search of food, they sometimes lie in wait, in the plains, or beside streams or patches of water, to catch man or beast.

The natives of those days believed that those huge reptiles were favoured by the great evil spirit which they worshipped; believing also in a good spirit, who would not injure them or deprive them of their food. Therefore, before venturing on their fishing parties, they used to place some of the old men, and those accused of witchcraft, near the haunts of those serpents, to propitiate their aid in obtaining their supplies of food during the winter season.

The new colonists were, many years ago, frequently carried off by these reptiles, until their firearms and united force nearly destroyed them. An odd one was still occasionally seen, but always attacked, and, if possible, destroyed.

We sailed on the 13th, and in a few days crossed the Line ; and it was fortunate for the lives of the horses that we did so, for there were thirty-two of them pent up in the hold, as close as they could be, and the heat told greatly upon them. One died, and some others were very ill. The vicious ones were completely subdued, and gave no further trouble.

On the 17th we got five degrees over the Equator, with a fresh breeze, when another horse died ; but as we got into the cooler climate, the rest became better.

We continued our voyage for some time, nothing particular occurring ; but the sharks about the ship were more numerous than ever I remember : they probably smelt the horses. The youngsters, on one occasion, lost their mess, by a large shark raising himself so far out of the water as to seize their mess of pork hanging near the sea by a string to soften it. The young men became infuriated, and begged hard for another portion ; on receiving which, they lowered it to the beast, who was recognized by a part of the string from his jaws. Nothing loth, he swallowed the bait, and was at length brought on board ; and on being opened, their rations appeared quite whole, and apparently nothing the worse. It was cooked, and reported excellent.

On the 27th, we made Ceylon; and on the 3rd August, Madras. We landed the thirty horses, by aid of the Masulah boats, next day, very thin, but in good spirits; and I delivered them to the commissary of ordnance, with great joy to myself, and got some credit for these horses, they being the first batch, on trial, from Sydney that had succeeded in reaching India.

After visiting some old friends, I embarked for Calcutta, where I arrived, without accident, on the 22nd, having been two years and five months from my duty on sick-leave. Here I received letters from my commanding-officer, Colonel Oglander, an excellent officer and right good man, stating that he was on his way with the 26th Regiment, accompanied by a wing of the 11th Light Dragoons, three native regiments, and six 12-pounders, to attack Joudpoor, the capital of a Rajpoot State, which had risen in rebellion, plundering neighbouring states, and committing many enormities.

I had nothing for it, if I wished to be up in time for fighting, but to go post to Ajmeer, a fatiguing journey of about eight hundred

miles, in a palanquin. It was now the beginning of September, the monsoon just commencing; so the sooner I started the better.
A few days I was obliged to wait, in order
to lay my palanquin-bearers; then off before
a week passed. The monsoon visited the
country with great fury,—so much so, that
I was detained in a post bungalow for two
days, and then made but short progress, being
often stopped by swollen rivers, inundations, &c.
An officer of the 26th (Captain Thompson)
travelled post with me, which was some
consolation on my dreary route.

It was not before the beginning of October
that we got to our destination, where we heard
that the rajah had submitted on seeing we
were in earnest. The force under Colonel
Oglander halted, and we had plenty of time
to join. Captain Thompson and I were very
much annoyed at seeing all our labour and
expense in vain, and agreed that, could we
have laid hands on his highness, we should
have been delighted to have obliged him
to partake of the whole of a bottle of
Chili vinegar — a dose that, without particularly injuring the man, would undoubtedly
have given him a very disagreeable employment
for some days.

The expedition against this troublesome prince being broken up, the different regiments proceeded to their several stations; we to Meerut, one of the best in this part of India —a few marches from the far-famed Delhi, Agra, the Tatz Mahal, &c.

All those eminent places have recently been so often described by travellers, that it is unnecessary, at this time of day, to attempt a description of them.*   Steam has brought distant countries so near, that travellers of the olden day have but little to say.   However this may be, a visit from the far West must still prove highly interesting, not only to witness those places so celebrated in history, both for good and evil deeds, but to enjoy a tour in the mighty Himalayas,† one of the grandest scenes in nature.

During the cool months, many of us got leave to visit those regions, or elsewhere, for sporting, the jungles in the neighbourhood

---

* My thirty years' service in most parts of the world is now quite out of date : the modern excursionists, of some three years' travel, cut me out.

† I first saw them at a great distance.   I felt astonishment, mixed with admiration.   The sight seemed to carry me to the Creator, to whom nothing is elevated, nothing is boundless.

of Meerut, at this period, teeming with game, particularly at many miles' distance, in the Cauder-Doon, extending a great way into the interior of deep jungle, and in former times being partly a bed of the mighty Ganges, before a sinking of the earth, or earthquake, elsewhere, caused it to flow in another direction.

The Cauder-Doon was then highly prized for its abundance of large game: various kinds of deer, the wild boar, and sometimes the elephant, were to be met with; and, above all, the tiger, of the largest and most ferocious kind, was here. There were some of the boars so large and determined, that some native hunters said they would face the tiger, meeting him in open field. This seldom occurred: the stealthy tiger, with all his ferocity, is cowardly in his ways; avoids open attack, preferring to advance under cover, and so surprise his enemy, springing upon him, and giving his mighty blow, which generally destroys his victim.

In many parts of the Doon are deep pools of water: some are occasionally covered with the lotus, red and white—very beautiful,—and huge creepers. In these lie the greenish species of alligator, a small but very dangerous and active kind, which in the evening lie on the edge of those pools, ready to seize any animal coming to drink.

Some parts of the Doon grow very beautiful shrubs and flowers,—amongst them a sort of dwarf rhododendron, yielding a strong perfume of rather an overpowering nature.

CHAPTER VI.

1835.

IN the early part of 1835, four of us, officers of the 26th, got leave of absence to visit the Doon for sporting; and then I had leave to proceed on a tour to the Himalayas. We procured four elephants, two of them steady animals, well used to sporting excursions. As we resolved to beat up large game, we agreed to begin about daylight, charged with ball in our rifles and double-barrels; and then, about noon, try for smaller game, which latter we were always sure of getting; and in the evening returning to our camp with a good bag, comprising some peafowl and an odd deer or two; florican, delicious eating; black partridge, snipe, &c.; and now and then a woodcock, in appearance resembling those in Europe.

How those birds of passage find their way to such an immense distance from where they breed, in Europe, is somewhat surprising. Peafowl, we found, made excellent soup, the flavour of which was superior to most others.

When we got a young one, we had him stuffed and roasted, turkey fashion, which did very well, for our Indian cooks were of the best.

Two hogs fell to our guns, but as yet no tiger. At last we got one. It was getting towards 12 A.M. one day, when about separating for small game, that a Royal tiger started up from the low grass between Captain Campbell's elephant and mine. The elephants shied, yet, considering the nearness and suddenness of the roar of the tiger, behaved well, for they were instantly brought up by the mahouts. The tiger, who stood his ground, made an attack on Campbell's elephant, but, by the management of the driver, he failed in reaching the howdah. Then we saw, by the waving of the grass, that he was creeping to a hollow full of trees at no great distance. Now, then, was our time. Before reaching the hollow, he was obliged to pass some bare ground; we were within about sixty yards of him, on this open space, when he turned to charge. We both fired with decided effect, one ball piercing his neck, the other ball breaking his shoulder-joint. How he could possibly rush forward, after receiving those fatal shots, surprised us; but he did so, and fell, to rise no more, close to our elephants. He was a very fine animal, six feet in length, not including the tail, which was nearly three and a half feet long, and the skin beautifully marked,—so much so, that we remained on the spot until two camel-drivers skinned him for us.

The inhabitants of the neighbouring villages came about us, rejoicing at their deliverance from an enemy who had not only killed several of their cattle, but two of themselves. And here I beg to say, with all due respect to brother sportsmen, that I have been not a little surprised in reading the facility with which they appear to destroy, in a given time, so many wild beasts at the present day—elephants, lions, panthers, &c. &c., in Africa, and tigers in India. · I can answer for the difficulty and danger of attacking the latter, particularly on foot or horseback. The wily and treacherous nature of those animals is proverbial—alas! to the cost of a very fine and most promising officer, Lieut. MacMurdo, of the Bombay Artillery, who went after a Royal tiger,* alone, and on foot. He found him, and on this occasion the tiger must have faced him; he waited his approach, until within some ten

---

* A man-eater is so called, from having killed and eaten several men.

paces, when he fired, just as the brute sprung forward. They were both found dead together, the officer from his head being crushed in by the tiger's blow, and the latter with a rifle-ball in his brain. Such was the account given by the deceased officer's horse-keeper, who watched the event from a prudent distance.

The term of leave of my companion-sportsmen having . expired, I proceeded alone to Delhi. On my way to the far-famed Himalayas, at Delhi, I met with an old friend in the Civil Service, holding a high position at the king's court, to whose house I went for the few days I intended to remain. He showed me over this celebrated place, and said, " If you stay here until the king holds his court, I will introduce you." On the day appointed, I accompanied my friend and suite to court. At the entrance to the state-rooms we were provided with a stuffed white silken slipper, in lieu of our boots; these were very comfortable and warm, as we threaded the marble floors. When. arrived in the throne-room, we saw a splendid muslin curtain, dividing it in the centre, before which we arranged ourselves according to our official rank, when we were offered iced water and fruit; and when we had partaken of these, the attendants withdrew,

I

and shortly after the curtain was drawn from its centre gently aside, and there, on his crystal throne, sat the king, a very fine-looking man, of middle age, surrounded by his court and some neighbouring princes to do him homage.

We all followed the example of the Resident, by bowing low, as we advanced towards him, three times. Our names and designation were stated to him by an emir, on his knees, holding up his hands in the most graceful manner possible (Asiatic fashion); another great man then brought in dresses of honour (khilauts), a sort of long flowing robe, which was thrown around each of us, and fastened on the breast by the king, who called each a Sahib Behauder.* We then retired, fronting the throne, when the curtain gradually closed, and so the reception ended.

This ceremony was certainly done extremely well: the very handsome fine-dressed men around the king, the old ones in muslin robes, many of the young ones, as a body-guard, in bright chain armour of gold and silver; the veneration and profound respect in their every look and demeanour, were certainly very grand and imposing. Alas for this unfortunate

* Title of nobility.

prince! for I believe him, from his great age, to be the same who, some twenty years after our introduction, lost even this semblance of power, and became an exile from his throne, being the leader in that terrible mutiny amongst the Company's sepoys in 1857.

But to resume. My route from Delhi to Simla, our sanitary station on the Himalayas, was full of interest; the beauty of the scene, joined to the fine bracing air as I ascended the hills, made me feel quite another man. The languor of the plains, in the feeling caused by the excessive heat, was forgotten in the enjoyment of a better climate.

Simla, as may be supposed, is a very gay place; hither the residents in the plains resort during the hot seasons, from the Viceroy downwards; and agreeable parties take place every evening, when dancing and other amusements are kept up until a late hour. The ladies of sober age ride about the vicinity of the station, while others keep moving about in their tomjohns, a sort of sedan-chair carried on men's shoulders; but what a little startled me was, young ladies galloping their goants, or hill ponies, on the narrow roads out on the sides of the mountains, some of them barely more than three-and-a-half feet wide, on one side a beetling cliff, hundreds of feet high, beneath them ; depths of sheer descents, called cuds, five hundred or a thousand feet down, where the least trip or unsteadiness of the pony must result in hurling them to destruction. However, as there is nothing in these cases like being used to things, so these extremely long-backed ponies, with very short legs, never, or very seldom, miss their footing; and away the girls go, along those narrow ways, in right good humour, screaming with laughter.

On my first going on them, I felt a little squeamish, for my Arab did not half like the space beneath, and at one time trembled much; I, however, encouraged him. He was one of the smallest of his kind, and knew me well,—he had stopped; but after a time I got him to go on. As turning round, without the chance of going down the cud, was all but impossible, I went on until I came to a turn in the mountain road that at length brought me to Simla. I met some ladies, who were surprised at my venturing on horseback, and begged I would not do so again; reminding me of the fate of Major Blundell, of the 11th Light Dragoons; which was this. He was riding along one of those narrow ways, not on a horse, but on a hill pony, when, in a cleft of the mountain, on his right, the head and neck of a large snake showed itself suddenly in front of his pony. The animal, frightened, turned outwards, missed his footing, and went down the fearful precipice full six hundred feet, and was dashed to pieces on the rocks below. The poor major's remains were picked up, mangled in a frightful manner.

Here I had the pleasure of meeting my old friend, Sir Charles Metcalfe, Lieut.-Governor of the Upper Provinces of this (at that time) remote part of India, sent by the Governor-General to arrange by arbitration some serious differences as to territory between the native princes and the Honourable Company, which were very near leading to a war, had not his great ability and thorough knowledge of the native character prevented it. The active and constant exertions of this great man brought on fever, and he was ordered by his doctors to Simla, to recruit his health.

Here I also met another friend, before mentioned, the Baron Hügell, exploring for native samples of vegetation, which he hoped to meet in abundance upon those mountains. I also met. another traveller, Major Jones, who had been in some parts of South Africa, in which land he had added but little to his stock, for the study of naturalists in England. He was not at all satisfied with his trip there, saying that for the most part the interior of this part of Africa was a disagreeable, barren waste, full of noxious reptiles, and tribes of people, savage, superstitious, and unnatural to the last degree. The Fans are particularly noted for giving to other tribes their own dead bodies, in exchange for theirs, for the purpose of eating.* They have children as wives at from eight to ten years of age, thereby for the most part destroying their powers of becoming mothers.

In this most agreeable place I remained three weeks, every day enjoying the delightful society of Sir Charles Metcalfe, and dancing with the girls in the evening; and as I was going to fall in love with one of them, I thought it best to continue my travels, which I did immediately.

Having laid in a good stock of provisions, on a couple of ponies, ammunition, &c., I started, going from eight to twelve miles a day. The road to Hotoo, nearly a hundred miles from Simla, was tolerably good. It was made by the corps of Gorka Pioneers, smart, good little

---

* M. De Chaillu, in his book on South Africa, mentions this horrible practice.

workmen, a hardy race that will do anything, from fighting to tiger-hunting.

The natives settled here from the plains disappeared a few marches from Simla, and I was now amongst the aboriginal inhabitants of these regions. As is usual amongst Highlanders, they appeared a stronger and more athletic race than those I left behind me. They were very civil and obliging, and freely gave me a small space in their huts, during my stay, wherever I happened to put up. Their clothing appeared to be a wrapper, made of a sort of thick Welsh flannel, but manufactured by themselves; a cap on their heads of the same material, and sandalled shoes, or slippers. Males and females wore much the same clothing. Their customs in married life are somewhat curious; and the great fall of snow and the severity of the climate sometimes completely isolate them from communication with neighbouring districts; so they collect a quantity of food during the summer months, for winter store; but in the higher land they are often shut up so long that starvation stares them in the face.

Tracts of table-land, more or less extensive, are covered in the season with vegetation, which must last all the year round; as it is on this

land they have their villages, under a head
man, or Thakoor, a sort of feudal chief, independent of all around him. The uncertainty
of feeding the inhabitants of any one of these
places is so great, that it obliges them not to
increase or multiply; so they have, from a
remote period, been accustomed to a species of
polygamy totally different from what that means
in other parts of the East. It is this. The females
have from two or three up to seven husbands
each. These husbands may be nearly related,
even be brothers. They have each a separate
hut, and one for a certain time remains at home,
while the others are employed in cultivating
their plots of ground or other work, principally
in gathering fuel for the winter. The children
born of this wife are recognized as near relations to all the husbands. They all appeared
quite satisfied with each other, neither did
there appear the least jealousy or disquiet
among them. Many people may think, from
this extraordinary arrangement, that they are
debauched and profligate. They are not at all
so, their habits appearing entirely owing to the
circumstances in which they are placed. The
mothers are kind and most affectionate to their
children, who are healthy and interesting in
appearance; and I have often looked at them,

watching the repose of a child arrived at the age of two years or so. These they place on a small mossy bank, under a little stream of water, which runs through a hollow stick, or bamboo, gently on the brow of the child. This, they told me, strengthens the head, in order to endure the severity of the cold winter.

My time was usually passed in shooting-excursions, where I found pheasants or other birds, and deer tolerably plentiful, and, if accessible to get, I generally remained a few days, giving, for the most part, what I got to the people amongst whom I lived. As I was furnished with my tackle, book of flies, and portable rod, I often fished in the pools and got a kind of trout, and small but good eels and dace, which the natives like better than any other food.

In some of the very deep pools they sometimes succeed in catching a very large fish, and from a specimen I saw, I conceived it was something of the sturgeon tribe.* These are invariably smoked, and preserved for winter fare.

Throughout my stay with those civil, and I may say, simple hill tribes, I saw nothing of impropriety at any time in their conduct.

On arriving at Hotoo, I found myself in the

* The mâshir are much of the same kind of fish, caught in the Ganges, near these mountains.

vicinity of eternal snow, and the chill at night was so great, that I had a fire at the entrance of my hut, which was kept up by one of the hill-men, to whom I gave a small gratuity in the morning : without this fire my four blankets would have been insufficient to prevent suffering from cold.

The small brown, and a kind of white pheasant smaller still, I found in tolerable abundance ; but my chief aim was to obtain the superb blue-and-golden pheasant called the Manaul.* This bird was very shy, and, from the localities they inhabit, difficult to approach ; their food being a sort of mulberry in the lower hills during winter, and a berry growing on dwarfed shrubs on the snowy heights in summer, resembling the wild sloe.

My two hill-men said, the only way I could possibly succeed in getting a shot at them, was by ascending a height of about three thousand feet and there concealing myself until daylight : this was to be done by pushing on my way up soon after midnight, to be in time for the birds. My hill-men accompanied me with blankets and some refreshment, and, after a very fatiguing and often difficult march, we arrived at the desired locality.

* A name appertaining to royalty.

The cold was great, but a nip of brandy made us feel somewhat comfortable. My men excavated with their forked poles a hole for me to lie in, against the wind blowing rather fresh from the S.E. As the scent of the Manaul is very keen, and should they suspect anything they would not approach their favourite food, which lay in plenty on the thick shrub about me, I waited here more than an hour, gun in hand, and blanket around me; the men had retired to a good distance below.

Daylight had not long appeared, when I heard a heavy whir of wings. They were what I wanted, and as two of them flew within thirty yards from me, I fired, with difficulty using my hand, being nearly chilled with cold; down dropped one, the other was hit, yet not enough to bring him down close, but he fell near enough for my men to see and find him. It was the male bird, and the finest specimen possible; in full plumage and of exquisite beauty, the size of nearly a full-grown peacock. The one that fell near me was the female, but neither in size or beauty like the male. I felt proud of my prize, resolving to preserve the skin. It was the first I had ever seen, and few Europeans at the time had seen them. In these days, however, they are occasionally met with preserved in museums, in all their gorgeous beauty.

As I had, *pro tem.*, finished preserving the skin of this celebrated bird, I began to retrace my way back to Simla, and as a few marches brought me to the vicinity of all the beauty of these regions, I was resolved to give up sport of all kind, and resign myself to the contemplation of them, and to put down all I could relative to their manifold excellence, which would indeed require one more capable than myself to express in any manner whatever.

Let those who love to contemplate the sublimity and grandeur of Nature, stand on the summit of one of those mountains and look around at the magnificent prospect revealed to them. The scene itself fills the mind with awe and wonder, and for a time all else but their contemplation is forgotten, as one gazes on the gigantic precipices, the valleys running down from them so deep that they become lost in their profundity to observation, and so grotesque are sometimes the appearances around, and so still, that one may fancy he sees the mighty ruins of a depopulated world. Then, again, the waterfall, more or less extensive, comes thundering in mighty grandeur from above, and gradually disappears in the forest below.

Many of the highest peaks,* covered with eternal snow, raise their heads even above the passing clouds to heaven, even as it is imaged in fabled history the Titans did of old.

The feeling of the spectator, I think, is no holiday one. It is not the place for an every-day man, who sets out on his tour to this part of the world to shoot down everything he fancies, and then, when tired, to see what comforts he can get in the way of food and rest, to gratify the appetites of the inner man. The wonders around me impressed my mind with a feeling somewhat related to the ever-lasting powers of the Great Eternal.

The murmuring sound of the huge dark pines;† the rhododendrons, in their bright pink flowers of enormous size; the palm, the fern, the myrtle, and other flowering trees and shrubs, all on a grand scale, were marvellously beau-tiful. Then, again, as you proceeded, villages around, on isolated pieces of table-land, with

---

* With my sextant I attempted to take the height of the highest peak, aided with an artificial horizon, and found it about 30,000 feet above the plains.

† Some of those pines are from 30 to 45 feet in circum-ference, and, could they be brought to the plains, would realise a large fortune.

dark-green cypresses marking the last resting-place of the dead.

On another occasion I waited till the sun had set, and then, throned in the western sky, the soft and silver moon rose in all its brightness, entirely changing the scene, and lighting up with magical effect the shadows thrown around, even unto the eastern sky, which it made appear in lurid flame, at times bursting on the sight, until a passing cloud darkened the evening luminary; then the monkey tribe and other animals ceased their hum, and, with the feathered race, retired to their repose; and as the night drew on, this unsurpassed scenery gradually faded from my view.

Thus I only enter into a hasty description of some of the sights of the Himalayas. My time of leave was expiring, and it was necessary to be present with my regiment before the next muster-day. I accordingly started on horseback for Simla, but was very often obliged to dismount and walk, or rather scramble, up or down heights or depths, having returned in a different direction to the one we came up by; one of my hill-men assisting me, the other man helping my little active Arab, which I nearly lost, he having missed his footing in a steep descent, and rolled down about thirty feet, but was luckily brought up by a thick patch of bushes, where the intelligent animal lay still until I and the two hill-men reached him. We then ascended by another path. The horse escaped with some bruises; limbs all right; bridle and saddle broken, and the man's arm dislocated in trying to hold him on from falling.

Thus we journeyed through continued fine and ever-varying scenery everywhere around us, sometimes through difficult and dangerous ways. In five days we again made the road to Simla, and proceeded with more comfort on our way; in another week we descried this rapidly-rising and beautiful settlement, where my old friend awaited me, cordially wishing me joy on my return in good health and spirits, and escorting me to his kind and comfortable home.

In this uncertain world, nothing, I think, can well be more happy than the life people lead at Simla. It is real luxury indeed, compared to that luxuriance and indolence of life at Calcutta, the latter habit caused by the intense heat. Every appliance that the native servant can bring to bear to relieve the oppression felt by Europeans is done there for their comfort, but it too often falls short to alleviate the sufferings of the invalid or the delicate, who so often fall victims to it.

At Simla the old Indian is blessed with a climate in temperature equal, if not in many cases superior to, England, coupled with the great beauty of an Eastern clime. The walk before breakfast is delightful, from the air of the neighbouring mountains, and one returns to breakfast with an English relish for it. The laugh of pretty and amiable women is delightful; and after ample justice is done to a breakfast partaking of all the good things of the East and the West, the amusement and occupation for the day are discussed. Some remain, and read the latest publications to the ladies; others betake themselves to billiards; while others take the gun to seek after partridge or quail, the last of which are abundant about the gardens and plantations. The ladies often feel sorry for their friends not being present to enjoy their happiness, and say, " Poor Mrs. So-and-so! how happy she would be among us, and what a relief it would prove to her poor delicate husband, wearied out with his troublesome duties on the Plains! But it will be their turn to be up here next year."

People in England little understand why old Indians enjoy each other's society so much when at home, and talk so much of the East. To me, as one of them, I think it extremely natural that they should be glad to meet, and talk over the many happy days they have spent there, so far away from friends and home. Yes, all the sterling good feeling possessed by the English character is in the East displayed to the best advantage. We there all know each other, and by every means in our power render mutual kindness. It is there often the only comfort we have on meeting together in stations burthened with intense heat, and but too often with hot suffocating winds, which, whirling and circling round, blow so terrific, that the house or bungalow you reside in is in part blown down, or unroofed; but at hill stations, or at delightful Simla, we have a superior climate, enjoyable in every sense of the word, together with nearly all the good things of the East, and the substantial comforts of Europe; the fruits surpassing in flavour those in the latter part of the globe; for instance, the mango, the pine apple, the plantain, the pomegranate, the custard apple, &c. Then, too, we have grown here delicious grapes, such as at home. In living we conform more to the way there, than we can conveniently do in the plains; we still ask our friend to take wine here, instead

K

of beer, which latter we find so strengthening below; we have the curious and fairy scene of fire-flies, as in the plains, at evening time; they flit about the tall dark branches of the pine, lighting up one spot for a short time, then off in a perfect cloud to another, and as night closes, resting on some favoured spot, and so disappear until the evening of the following day.

Those interesting little creatures are perfectly harmless, neither do they plague you, like other numerous insect tribes,* which in the plains are so tormenting, particularly when your candles are lit, which without protection are covered with flying ants, and put out by their slaying themselves by hundreds.

The fire-fly is less in size than our common black fly, and loses in great part its luminous appearance when looked at in the hand; its phosphoric ·power ceases until it regains its freedom, when it becomes as usual a fire-fly.

The *tout ensemble* of Simla and its vicinity

---

* It has often surprised me that naturalists have not accounted how it happens that the white ant, which is a small, soft insect, can, by vast numbers, under the cover of earth conveyed upwards by them, destroy everything in their way but metal. I had thirty books destroyed in four hours.

brought me back to England.   It reminded me
of the fine park scenery round Eridge Castle,
and other old places at home, with its open
and impressive landscape; aided by the great
additional grandeur of the lofty trees of various
kinds, and shades surrounding, or occupying
the ground in groups at distant glades : then
in the distance again, but only through a glass,
the far off forest, sloping off towards the
plains, was sublime.   On riding about, I would
sometimes fancy that gold and green were the
livery of nature.   Throughout the year chry-
santhemums of great beauty, and other flowers
almost constantly blooming, and the white
crocus, occasionally succeeded by the blue, in
all their simplicity ; roses, too, were everywhere
in blossom ; but I missed the sweet-smelling,
lovely cabbage-rose of England, and the moss-
rose, so exquisite, was unknown.   Jessamine on
a large scale was here, but not with its European fragrance ;   the myrtle, gigantic and
abundant.

Some recent settlers have brought out with
them from England flower seeds of various
kinds; amongst those now grown are the
carnation and mignonette.   They seemed to
thrive, but are yet in their infancy; time, however, and culture, will no doubt produce them

in perfection, as they have succeeded in doing with other productions of plants and seeds of Europe in this favoured climate.

Those regions possess also, as well as the plains, a full share of beautiful birds, some with white bodies and light blue wings, with bands of a dark hue; green paroquets in abundance, rushing about with sharp cries; the pretty yellow and black mangoo-bird; doves, cooing their love all day long, with the bulbul,* and, indeed, an endless variety.

On the ground, or up the trees, grey squirrels chased each other about without fear, and in their eagerness to catch each other, springing from bough to bough, sometimes missing their hold and tumbling downward, but always saving themselves by catching some foliage in their descent.

The native servants who accompanied us to the hills did not much relish the cold of the night, and preferred the plains; they all brought with them curry, and prepared their rice as usual. How pretty many of the Hindoo girls look, when going to or returning from the wells with water! They all go in file, that is, all in a row, following their leader, with their

* Indian nightingale.

water chatty or jug poised on their heads, ascending or descending the slopes of the path-
way, their interesting figures moving tranquilly
along, chatting or often chaunting their village
love-ditty.

CHAPTER VII.

1835.

AFTER a week's residence here, I was on the point of starting for my regiment, when I received a letter from Colonel Oglander, to say that I had been promoted and had a year's leave granted me, in order to return to England.

I had plenty of time to do what I had long wished for, and that was, to visit the Punjaub, go to Lahore, the capital, and see the lion of the North, the great Runjeet Singh, our ally. I had become acquainted with two Sindars, officers of rank in this sovereign's service, and to my request, that I might be permitted to join them on their way to Lahore, they courteously consented. A couple of days were enough to make my arrangements, and I left Simla with something like sorrow, for everything there agreed with my wishes to become a settler in those delightful hills. I parted with my kind friend, and all others who were kind to me, including Lady Sale, who on the death of her gallant husband was determined to end her days here.

We crossed the Sutlej river, which divided the Punjaub from our possessions, on rafts, constructed for the purpose, and saw good cultivation on its banks, but excepting there, a sandy, and with few exceptions, a barren country around. We travelled on horseback, at the rate of about twelve or fifteen miles a day, starting at about two every morning, for the plains here are sometimes as hot as they are in India proper.

We met, on our way, hill forts, apparently well garrisoned with Sikh soldiers. Our provisions were carried by tattoos, or baggage-ponies, an animal that seems never tired; the Sikh officers having curry stuff, and maize, which their attendants made into chupaties, or cakes; rice, and the small farm-fowls of the country they got at every village. These we bought at a dozen for a rupee, the villagers seldom taking payment from the officers.

The Sikhs* seem by no means so strict in their customs as the Hindoos; I believe, as soldiers particularly, they can eat fish and

* In appearance and strength they are far superior to the Hindoos.

flesh as they like, only paying their goorro, or
priest, a small recompense on confession.

I had with me only coffee, sugar, and a few
biscuits, living principally, as the others did, on
curry and rice, which was always excellent.
One of my fellow-travellers spoke a little
English, the other officer French, which, with
the aid of Hindoostani, made our time pass
well enough. Both were intelligent and merry
fellows; they recounted to me some clever and
indeed wonderfully skilful acts of their prince,
whom they compared, in his military successes,
to the great Napoleon, and saying that they
and the whole of his army would be but too
happy to lose their lives in his service.

As yet the scenery in this land was not equal
at all to what I left behind me; but still there
were some very good prospects occasionally,
and the cultivation of maize was abundant.
After several days' journey we came to some
very rapid streams, where, even at the fords,
three to four feet deep, our horses found it
most difficult to keep their feet. Many of
those rapid streams feed the great fine rivers
of this country, which our army, in 1838, found
it so difficult to cross on their way to Afghanistan, and in which we lost many men and
horses. There were not many large towns on

our route, but all showed a state of defence, with more or less soldiers.   It was thus Runjeet Singh provisioned his army, and when called upon to unite his forces, they generally assembled nearest the enemy to be attacked, and, joined by their chief and the European officers, manœuvred them for a time more or less, as the emergency required.   In this way, and by natural military tact and knowledge, this great Indian chief was enabled to conquer and rule with energy a mighty kingdom ; resembling the great master of Europe in one particular —the commencing his career from a humble station in life.

The peasantry appeared to have a general respect and fear of his name.   Marauders, when caught plundering them, were immediately punished, and sometimes hung.   The industrious and well-behaved were encouraged, and always rewarded when deserving of it ; neither were the Sikh soldiers permitted to take anything from them without payment, excepting in small matters of vegetables and fruit,* which were generally given to them voluntarily.   The rice grounds were not anything like so numerous as in most parts of India, but

---

* For everything else they offered payment.

over large tracts of country were grown millet and Indian corn.

We halted for a day or two occasionally, for the purpose of having shooting excursions. Quail we found sometimes in abundance, together with the sand grouse : this bird is rather less than a partridge, but better eating. They are pretty birds, of various dark and light hues, and are now getting well known; not so the spur fowl, a dark-brown mottled bird less than a grouse, with three sharp spurs on one leg, and four on the other. They are only found in certain tracts of dense cover, and so difficult to be made rise without dogs, that if they cannot get out of the way by swift running, will almost allow you to tread on them. They and quail are the most delicate eating birds in the East, except perhaps florican. This bird is now,. I suppose, well-known; it is beautiful, but rather stupid; after long flights it alights in grass, and is put up easily within shot. They vary in size and colour; light brown, speckled, dark, the largest; black, with white streaks, the smallest, and of bustard shape, of the size of hen pheasants, though some are much smaller.

We sometimes came on small antelope not much larger than a hare, which, when dressed and stuffed with fine herbs by the servants of

the Sikh officers, were excellent. We sometimes saw troops of jackals scouring over the
plains, and occasionally the pretty little red and
black fox : these we hunted with some dogs of
all kinds, and often killed after a run of ten or
a dozen miles. A wolf was now and then seen,
darker in hue than the usual kind. The Sikhs
have some curious traditions regarding those
animals, and stated that killing them on certain days was very unlucky. A curious sort
of wild hog was brought in to us one day, he
was of a dusky red colour, with a large muzzle
for a pig, and great bumps upon his head.
The natives had trapped him, and appeared to
consider his capture as quite an exploit; the
ugly brute being very pugnacious, and, if attacked, turning at once on its opponents, and
with its sharp tusks, two on each side of the
jaw, lacerating their legs, inflicting severe
wounds. This animal is much smaller and
more active than its tribe; it is of solitary
habits, living on roots, principally of an aro-
matic kind, in deep jungle, and never seen in
herds.

We had some steaks cut from it, but the
taste was so musky, that we did not relish it;
my Hindoo servants, however, were not so nice,
for they soon disposed of the flesh in curries,

which ate better, but still had a disagreeable flavour. Another day, the natives brought to us a very large armadillo; in shape it was more like a huge lizard than a hog, was upwards of two feet in length and eight inches in breadth, covered with tortoise-shell scales of a dusky white colour. His captors saw a pile of earth moving, poked it with their sticks, and felt the animal below, under a heap of red ants; he was on his back, and nearly motionless when captured. This extraordinary animal, on finding an ant-heap, his favourite food, forces his way underneath; then, turning himself on his back, devours the ants as they attack him, until his appetite is satisfied. This one appeared to have either gorged himself into a state of stupor, or else the ants had succeeded in stinging him nearly to death, for they appeared to have entered his body by a small fracture in one of the joints of his shell, and thus revenged themselves upon their enemy. I had some difficulty in getting the body out, so as not to injure its shape; this was accomplished after some time, and the shell entire was a capital specimen of its kind.

I had heard so much of the dexterity of the Sikhs on horseback, that I mentioned my desire to witness it to my fellow-travellers, and

they at once kindly agreed to show me some on
the next halting-day. When this came, they
had their pretty Arabs made ready for the occasion. Their first exploit was riding at the
ring, as with us, but with far more speed; at a
ring not much larger than an eyeglass, which
they always carried off on their spears. They
then tied a mango, suspended from a tree, biting
a piece of it out with their teeth, when passing
it at speed. Then they stuck pegs in the
ground somewhat firmly; these they succeeded
in raising with the spear, their person bent
down, and spears grasped in the centre, hori-
zontally, horse in full gallop.

Then they betook themselves to their matchlocks—weapons splendidly carved and gilded;
setting bottles down, at which they rode at
full speed, and when within about fifty yards
fired at and broke, not missing once in six
discharges. Let the reader think how difficult
this was to do: the match brought down by a
trigger to an aperture in the breech communi-
cating with the charge, and, with a single ball,
seldom missing the object fired at.

But their last and still more wonderful feat
was performed by an instrument, in shape like
a quoit, which they generally carry in their
head-dress; but it is twice as large, and made

thinner, the outer edge sharpened, keen as
their swords. A palanquin-pad was placed on
an upright bamboo stick, the height of a man
on horseback. The performer then came forward, placing this singular weapon on the
fore-finger of his left hand, spinning it round;
and, when reaching a certain velocity, seizing
it with the finger and thumb of his right hand;
and hurling it at the pad, which it cut in two
parts, the instrument twirling back and falling
near the thrower: this also was done on horseback, but at rest, the distance about thirty-five
yards. This put me in mind of what I saw
done with the boomerang, in Australia, in other
days, now no doubt well known. This weapon
the Australian threw with great accuracy at
his adversary, and so contrived was it as to
come bounding back to the thrower. The quoit
affair, however, of the Sikh officer was by far
the most surprising and expert.

The Irregular Horse, which, as already mentioned, I had charge of in the Deccan, were
nearly all very active, and well versed in the
system of attack and defence; for instance, they
used to ride at each other at speed, using their
small rope bridles only, and quick as thought
cut them asunder. This puts me in mind of
the duel of the late Sir Thomas Dallas of other

days, who upon hearing that the native chiefs
of Hyderabad had declared they would meet
any British officer on horseback singly, accepted
the challenge, and was immediately answered
by several of them. One, however, was selected.
The morning of the fight was fixed upon; swords
only were to be used, in which Sir Thomas was
singularly expert. On the day fixed a number
of British officers, including the celebrated Sir
John Malcolm, assembled, with a host of native
chiefs, on the ground appointed. The com-
batants approached each other at about three-
quarter speed, and commenced by numerous
feints to deceive each other in attack. They were
both armed with the peculiar scimitar used by
Mussulman horsemen, of which Sir Thomas
was as much master as was his skilful opponent.
At the close of an attack by the latter, Sir
Thomas threw forward the chief's horse, slightly
wounding his bridle hand; but in this critical
moment the chief succeeded in cutting in two
Sir Thomas's bridle, which left him defenceless,
with the exception of his holster pistol, which in
the excitement of the moment he at once fired,
and again wounded the chief. Thus ended this
remarkable single combat; so like the chivalry
of the olden times. It appeared afterwards
that an objection was made to Sir Thomas

using fire-arms, but others were of opinion that the chief acted first unfairly, in cutting the gallant knight's horse's bridle. Be this as it may, there was not much harm done, as the wounds of the chief were not of so serious a character as to prevent his perfect restoration to health.

Some of my Irregular Horse, all Mussulmen, were exceedingly clever with their favourite weapon, the scimitar, sharpened to the keenness of a razor. For instance, one of them would remain stationary, holding in his hand a small pad of hair, or feathers, sometimes an orange, while another would approach him at speed ; when close, the pad or orange was hurled at the rider, who invariably cut it in two. In the use of the spear or matchlock, they did very well, but could never for a moment cope in the use of either with the Sikhs.

I have heard that, in these days, that description of cavalry either do not practise those beautiful feats on horseback, or they attend more in feats of arms to the steady and uniform discipline of the sword or spear of our time. However, I may as well mention, that the Kaffirs of Africa are very adroit in the management of their favourite weapon, the assaigais, as I witnessed, I think, at Graham's Town ; and their war-dance, previous to beginning, appears to the European, very ludicrous. Two of these warriors approached us to exhibit, assegais in hand; they were nude, with the exception of a fine grass-worked girdle round their loins, and a kind of cap on their heads of the same material, high, like our grenadier cap, but of the same breadth from top to bottom, which caused it to look very queer.

They neared each other, raising their legs occasionally and slapping their thighs; then, suddenly bouncing round, with their backs to each other, appeared to make some degrading signs of contempt, &c.; they then hopped close to each other, bent down, and rubbed noses of amity. After their dance, they separated, and at about a hundred yards apart, marked, on the ground, two small bushes; then twirling their assegais upright, they spun them up high in the air, and both weapons came down at the same time, with the points in the centre of the marks. Again, twirling the assegais, but this time round their heads, they threw them forward into the trunk of trees which they had previously marked; first at fifty yards, then at a hundred, and last of all at one hundred and fifty yards distance, never once missing the mark. After this, they again had their war dance, but of a kind apparently of more triumph than when they began. We gave them a present, which they seemed to expect; and no doubt they were practised hands.

In relating the above exploits to my fellow-travellers in other parts of the world, they have been highly amused, as well as with my account of different incidents that I had known, relative to military matters in European warfare; and such was the good humour and agreeable bearing of my companions, and our days often passed so quickly, that we neared the completion of our journey without feeling in the least desirous to part, but rather the contrary.

A few days before reaching Lahore, we visited a large establishment for the manufacture of sugar, a very low-roofed building in the midst of extensive plantations of sugar-cane. The sugar-cane when ripe is cut down and crushed by means of a very simple process, something like what I saw in Hindostan, but on a more massive scale and improved principle. In several compartments round the building were large square stones, fixed in the ground, and hollowed within, three to four feet deep, and so constructed as to admit a large piece, or rather beam, of very hard rounded wood, at the same time leaving space in the cavity sufficient to contain a certain quantity of sugar-cane cut to the required size. To the upright part of the timber outside is affixed a rope, to which are yoked two oxen, who work it round, thereby crushing the cane placed therein. The juice flows through an aperture in the socket, to a trough running into an underground passage, and thence to a large earthen boiler, under which a fire is kept burning. When the sugar is sufficiently boiled, it is drawn into another vessel, where, before growing cold, it is cut into pieces of the size required for use.*

We at length arrived at early morning in the vicinity of Lahore, and as daylight appeared were agreeably surprised with the scene which burst upon our view. Far as the eye could reach, on the ample space around, were various groups and lines of the troops of Runjeet Singh, performing their exercises: some according to their own peculiar mode, others again appearing to drill after the European style of tactics, under the superintendence of French officers; artillery occasionally scouring over the plain, halting, giving fire, then off in another direction.

---

* Irrigation is carried on as it is in other parts of the East, and water raised by pulleys, either from deep wells, or retained for use, by large tanks of water, in valleys, sustained by strong-built bunds, or banks of earth or masonry.

It was yet early, and the sun just peeping in its glory over the lofty walls of Lahore, gave to view this extensive town, fortified by walls, generally in the usual native way; but some advanced work showed the skill of the European system, with cannon thereon, ready for any emergency. On drawing nearer, this place put me very much in mind, with its impressive scenery, of Hydrabad, in the Deccan, which in my time was very warlike in appearance, and in attitude more so, from its armed walls and imposing soldiers, ever bearing matchlock, tulwar, and dagger, and ever ready to fight. The sun rose, brilliant in dazzling whiteness, pouring his light through the crenelated openings of the fortress; and as we continued to gaze on this beautiful and imposing scene, a salvo of cannon of large calibre was fired in the distance, and soon after appeared some horsemen at a gallop, riding along the lines of soldiers. But who is that slight horseman at their head, on the beautiful milk-white steed? It is the sovereign—the "Lion of the Punjaub" —the justly-celebrated Runjeet Singh, inspecting his troops.

My companions, this morning, turned out in their uniforms—a padded tunic of fine dark cotton, with a silver-chain cuirass fastened thereon, a silver helmet, red trowsers and boots, and armed with sword and spear. I had on my old embroidered green frock-coat and gold-lace forage cap, my usual dress when in charge of my horsemen at Hydrabad.

In making his circuit, Runjeet Singh passed near enough for us to bend to our saddle-bows, the officers at the same time lowering their spears. The salute was acknowledged, and the chief passed to other parts of the field. As my fellow-travellers and I proceeded to the capital, we were met by many acquaintances of theirs, and greeted on a safe return home. Some old friends accompanied us to Lahore, and we mutually told the news of passing events to each other. At length we entered one of the principal gates, strongly built, and guarded by native soldiers armed with French muskets, and habited something like our native troops in India, but in place of red cloth had quilted white cotton jackets, made after the French pattern. They had black cross-belts and caps, in the Sikh fashion.

At this time the general-in-chief of Runjeet Singh was away. This officer was General Alard. He was much distinguished under the Emperor Napoleon, and had rendered important service to his present sovereign. In his absence he was succeeded by General Ventura, also distinguished under Napoleon. There were other veteran officers, both from the French and Italian armies of the late European war, who held command of brigades and regiments. They all spoke English, and the language of this country fluently.

We proceeded through the town, passing many well-built houses, and observed the streets better and much cleaner than generally met with in eastern countries. We stopped at the entrance of a large building, something native as well as European in fashion, and were met by the servants of the house, who seemed delighted at their master's return. On dismounting, we were ushered in, and instantly served with a cup of good hot coffee, cakes, and some excellent dried meat, in slices; a small, sweet, native liquor was added thereto; then a cigar was smoked, and then we were shown our apartments. They were of the usual kind—that is, large and open, lofty and well ventilated. After a good bath, I enjoyed rest and sleep until noon, when I prepared for dinner at two o'clock.

At the time appointed we assembled, and several other parties who dined together much in European fashion: they were mostly

officers of the army. This new custom was
introduced by the French officers, with the
wish of the sovereign, whose object it was to
bring them together, that they might freely
converse on professional matters. There was
also some ceremony in the order of sitting at
table, which was, that those highest in rank
should occupy the upper part, whilst the juniors
in rank sat at the bottom; this, I believe, is the
invariable custom of a French regiment: the
same etiquette is not observed with us.

I duly sent my address to court, and begged
the favour of an interview to pay my respects,
which was accorded, on a durbar day, when a
levee would be held for all those who had not
previously seen his Highness the Maharajah.
The appointed day arrived, and, dressed in my
green uniform, I accompanied my friends to
court. We were led through a long line of
officers and courtiers, filling various functions
of dignity and importance, nearly all dressed
in military fashion, and according to the arm
they belonged to; but all were most picturesque
and handsome. Some of the chiefs, in their
splendid chain cuirasses of burnished gold,
with their brilliant spiked or plumed head-
pieces, bore a most chivalrous appearance.
There were the European officers, in the

costume of their rank, and some wearing on their breasts the star of the brave, the far-famed Legion of Honour, which they had gained in many a hard-fought field. I was now before the great chief, in my turn, and on bowing low his Highness returned it, and motioned for me to approach him, when the following conversation passed :—

Runjeet Singh.—" You were in the great European war ? "

" Yes, your Highness."

" That ribbon on your breast shows you fought well ?"

" I have been fortunately considered as having done my duty."

" Where have you served ? "

" In Spain, Portugal, Holland, the Netherlands, and India."

" Ah! then you were under a great commander, the Duke of Wellington ? "

" I was."

" His army was well trained and very brave, and confident in his great talents; but I have heard that he much neglected them when peace was established ? "

I hardly knew how to answer this question. At length I said—

" At that time there were some very influential parties in England, who wished for a reduction of the army, as it was of great expense to the nation ; to this the government was obliged to agree."

The Prince (after a slight pause) said,— " England has proved itself one of the greatest of nations. I have always been on friendly terms with that country, and it has ever been kind to me."

The Rajah.—" Pray permit me to ask you, as a soldier, did your army wish the Emperor Napoleon to be sent into exile, when *la fortune de la guerre* [with much emphasis] placed him in your power ? "

This was another difficulty to answer.

" I am sure they did not ; neither had the army, to the best of my belief, a voice on the subject. The Emperor Napoleon was exiled by a predominant party in the government of the day, who perhaps thought it best to send him to an island well protected ; but I can of myself truly say that the regiment I belonged to looked upon it with a species of horror, but this feeling was only whispered amongst ourselves."

The sovereign then bowed, and I retired.

I felt much flattered by the notice his Highness was pleased to take of me, as I afterwards learned that his questions were by no means of an ordinary kind.   The prince had heard from my fellow travellers a good account of me, and I thought had formed a better opinion of my experience and knowledge than perhaps I deserved.   No doubt great men, being placed in an exalted position, ought to derive information on all subjects from all they chance to have communication with.   Runjeet Singh was ever anxious to learn the policy and character of other nations, as a guide to direct him in his intercourse with them; and his great sagacity enabled him always to be on friendly terms with England.

I was greatly struck with the appearance and energetic bearing of this great Eastern chief, who, although below the middle size of his countrymen, yet his person and face, notwithstanding the loss of an eye, were handsome and expressive in a high degree.   On returning, my comrades begged me to repeat to them what their chief had said, and then remarked to each other that doubtless his Highness would have been happy to have had me in his service.   /

I was treated extremely well during my stay with my Sikh friends, who got up many entertainments and amusements common to this country, such as short plays of a comic nature,

and sword fights, all in good temper. Their
music is better far than that of Hindostan, and
the female dance more lively, and of a more
moral kind. There were Circassians, Georgians,
Afghans, and other foreigners, all under sur-
veillance of a well-organized, well-paid military
police, who knew their business and where-
abouts. The Circassians and Georgians I saw
were handsome active-looking men, and their
eyes most expressive. There were also natives
from Cashmere, mostly merchants, with shawls
and scarfs of great request in the Punjaub.
Every Sikh officer had one, more or less costly,
which they either wore Highland fashion, over
the shoulder, or round the waist, like a sash,
with rich trimmings hanging below, which had
a very graceful effect. In their amusements
they had small French roulette-tables, billiards,
and games of odd-and-even, during leisure
moments. Gambling was prohibited, and if
discovered on any occasion, particularly amongst
the soldiers, was sometimes severely punished.
Some of the chiefs amused themselves with pet
quails, the males of which are very pugnacious
little birds. They are trained to run about a
table and fight each other, the issue of which
is looked to with considerable interest. Small
bets are made, openly, on the contest; but

I heard that sometimes heavy sums were risked (underhand) by wealthy men of high class.

The usual sporting parties were often formed, when the spear was used, as with us, in hog-hunting. The dexterity of the Sikh with this weapon was such that, single-handed, he would face a boar, and wound or kill him, without endangering his horse being ripped or wounded. Not so with us: we require aid to draw off the attention of the animal when brought to bay, without which many accidents occur, especially to the horses.

The religious tenets of the Sikhs I cannot say I became well acquainted with. I believe Hindooism, with some difference, is their creed; but they do not appear to observe the strictness or stringent rules of the Brahmin caste, although they do some of their customs. Polygamy is followed, but not so generally practised, except by the great men—the peasant or soldier having only one wife. The suttee, or burning of widows, goes to the extent of consuming several at the death of the prince they belong to; this practice does not, however, always follow.

I was once honoured with the sight of a friend's wife. She was a beautiful Georgian woman, quite as fair as an Italian lady. Her hands and feet were small, and extremely well formed.   She wore open-worked jewelled sandals, and had jewels in profusion on her well-shaped head, and wavy hair of great length about her shoulders.   She sang a pretty troubadour-like song, accompanying it on a species of guitar of a circular form, having many strings.   The tone was softer than our own, and perhaps more resembled the small Welsh harp of former days.   She was extremely fond of her husband, who spent all his leisure time with her.

I ventured to ask this interesting creature if she would burn with her husband, in case of his death; and she answered, without hesitation, that she would, for she loved him so much that she could not bear to be separated from him.   This couple were truly happy.   They appeared, for Eastern people, much above its prejudices.   The lady, too, had learned so much of the French language as to make herself easily understood.

The weather was very fine, sometimes very hot during the day; but the evenings were cool, and the refreshing breezes from the distant lofty mountains rendered the climate at most times temperate.   It was now getting on to the latter end of August, and drawing towards the time when Runjeet Singh's review of his army took place. From distant stations it was already on the march to the capital for that purpose. There was collected a large store of provisions, forage, and herds of cattle, in the vicinity of the camp now forming for the accommodation of the troops; the different pennons and flags, marking the several arms, whether of cavalry, artillery, or infantry, around, appearing in great numbers, and had a gay and striking effect upon the beholders. The coming review, then, was well worth my seeing, ere I bade a final adieu to my hospitable entertainers.

Some time after this, the Sikh army began to appear, and the officers, European and native, fully occupied in guiding them to their appointed stations. The cavalry were mounted on light active horses; the artillery horses were larger, and stronger built. This arm was peculiarly under the guidance of French officers, and appeared well trained. They had tumbrils and ammunition waggons, well supplied. The well-drilled regular infantry looked extremely well in their white costumes (European fashion), cross-belts, muskets, and bayonets, glittering in the sun. At length the whole disposable army of the state arrived, numbering some forty thousand cavalry, artillery, and infantry, stationed in or around Lahore.

The 2nd of September was the date decided on for the inspection by the sovereign, and it was to occupy three days : first day, the inspection of infantry ; second day, cavalry and artillery ; third day, the whole army was to be formed into close bodies of horse, columns of infantry, and batteries of artillery, to march past the Maharajah, right in front.

On the day appointed, at two in the morning, the infantry, in columns, formed to order, were assembled, and at daylight made a very handsome appearance. Directly the sun rose, a salute of heavy guns announced the approach of his Highness. His flag was mounted high in the centre before his army, to which he galloped with a numerous suite, which I was previously invited to join. Thus we followed the chief along and around the whole of the infantry, which he appeared attentively to inspect, their respective drums and bands playing his Grand March as he passed. This inspection lasted nearly four hours ; the Maharajah then galloped to the centre, and on a discharge of artillery being fired as a signal of dismissal, the whole marched off to their camps. Thus ended the first day.

On the second day, at the same hour in the morning, the neighing of horses proclaimed the advance of the cavalry, and the noise of wheels that of the artillery—upon the same ground, before occupied by the infantry. As the day broke, a salute, as before, told of the arrival of the chief. The cavalry were on the right, massed in quarter distance columns, and the artillery were massed in batteries to the left. As the Maharajah passed, the trumpets sounded war-like tunes, and I never saw native troops better appointed. The native cavalry of India were not better mounted, and they all looked right well and fit for service. The artillery seemed also in perfect order, but not having that splendid appearance that the European artil-lery has in India; indeed, I think the latter are the most perfect artillery in the world. This day's inspection was over before noon; and I was not sorry for it, as suddenly the sun burst out from a mass of clouds, upon our heads, burning hot. On his Highness retiring, the usual signal was fired, when the cavalry and artillery retired to their respective lines.

The third and last day was now to come, and we hoped for a cool day, such as we had had, for the most part, previously.

Soon after midnight the army began to march to their respective posts on the plains around, the officers explaining the orders they had received to their men regarding the brigades and regiments of regular infantry, of cavalry, artillery, and light or irregular horse, who were to pass in succession before his Highness the Maharajah, according to their rank and degree; and this arrangement was strictly attended to. As the day dawned, the sovereign was at his post, and a splendid sight indeed was before and around us. There was the whole army present, formed in masses something like three sides of an immense square, the artillery in the centre, extending some miles, all glittering, as the sun arose, in their best dress, and presenting, from their varied costume, one of the grandest and most picturesque sights I had ever seen. The bright steel head-pieces and chain cuirasses of the cavalry, with their spears erect—the infantry, with their bright barrels, shouldered arms, and fixed bayonets —the gorgeously-dressed chiefs and officers, formed a whole not to be surpassed of its kind anywhere.

The day commenced with a salute to the Maharajah of one hundred guns from the centre; the cavalry then advanced, and, when

near enough, wheeled to the left, and on they
came in quarter-distance column, right in front
of squadrons in which were one hundred men.
As they passed the Maharajah, the officers
saluted European fashion, to which his Highness bowed low in return.   There passed of
this arm something like eight thousand men;
then came on the regular infantry at quarter-
distance column, at quick time, with closed
ranks, keeping their appointed distance, and
well set-up and soldier-like in appearance they
were, the trumpets, drums, and bands of both
cavalry and infantry giving great effect to the
passing scene.   At length came the Sikh
Matchlock infantry, and, as they passed the
presence, gave a shout for the Maharajah,
shaking their matchlocks in the air.   The light
artillery passed on well at a canter; then came
the heavy artillery at a walking pace, and, as they
passed, struck up their wild kettle-drum and
trumpet music; last came the irregular horse,
as the day, which had been most favourable for
the review, was closing, and thus ended a spectacle most novel, and so chivalrous as to
remind one of the bygone feudal times amongst
ourselves; and as long as I exist in this frail
body I shall ever recollect with pleasure Runjeet
Singh's review of his army.   It is true I have

seen large European armies collected together, both for fighting and review, but the excitement produced by them was but tame and dull in comparison to what I have above so feebly described.

It was well for the army that the inspection here terminated, for the monsoon suddenly burst upon us with extreme violence,—so much so, that tents and huts were blown down in all directions, horses broke loose from their pickets, and galloped furiously about the country; and altogether the scene of confusion around was indescribable. So violent was the wind and rain, that most of the troops were obliged to seek shelter wherever they could, either in Lahore or the villages around. The men of the cavalry and artillery were miserably off, for they, in spite of wind and rain, were obliged to look after their horses. However, the Sikhs are a hardy race, and did not suffer so much as the Hindoos under like circumstances would have done, and, like good soldiers, secured their horses under any cover they could, so long as this terrible weather lasted. At the end of three days it moderated, and so much so, that matters began to get into order. The sun came forth, and enlivened us all. It was well that plenty of food and forage had been in store, as it enabled the almost famished men and horses to be served out with both. The effects produced by the storm passed rapidly away, and everything about the encampment resumed its order and regularity. In a few days it was finally broken up, when the army, separating, marched off to occupy their former stations.

The time was now approaching for my departure. I had a land journey before me, and a voyage to England to get over, before my leave expired. A Sikh officer offered me a good price for my pretty Arab, which I sold to him, knowing how well he would be cared for. Having sent in my name to the Maharajah in farewell, his Highness expressed a wish to see me. I accordingly waited on him, when he was pleased to express the satisfaction he felt at my having witnessed the review of his army, saying, " I know you will give your comrades a good account of it;" and then, throwing a rich yellow scarf over my shoulders, bade me farewell, and withdrew.

Alas! how a few years will alter everything. Here was a powerful state, formed by the genius of this great man, only to last with unexampled prosperity during his life. At his death, in a few years after my last interview, his successors got into difficulties with the English Government on two occasions.   On both sides war was declared, and after two hard-fought campaigns, and the loss of very many gallant men, the Sikh army in the last conflict was finally subdued, and the present heir to the Musnud, Maharajah Dhuleep Singh, is now residing in England, and a favourite at the Court of Queen Victoria.

The day previous to my departure I was visited by all those whom I became acquainted with here, who expressed themselves sorry I was leaving, wishing me all happiness through life. I gave them something as a remembrance; and my two late travelling companions begged my acceptance of a very handsome matchlock, to whom I presented my pistols in return, and so we bade adieu.   A farewell is always accompanied, more or less, with a feeling of melancholy, when parting from those we may never see again.

CHAPTER VIII.

1835.

ON the morning of the 12th of September I was on my way, and, as I passed across the plains, was gratified by the sight of, I suppose, nearly five hundred elephants, those used on state occasions, in their splendid appointments, but most of them belonging to the army, for service against the enemy in time of need. There are generally two attached to draw a heavy piece of artillery, which those intelligent animals become familiar with, and, without being led, proceed to it for the purpose of being harnessed before the time of march commences. In fact, by some training, and the kindness of their keepers, they can be made · to do anything wanted. This reminds me of their use in the siege of Asseerghur, in 1819. They not only dragged the breaching-cannon up the slopes of attack, but, when the ground was too steep for that, they were turned, two at a time, placed with their heads to the wheels, and so gradually forced them on to their respective platforms. The elephants I now saw were mustered for inspection by order of the Maharajah, and, as they passed the inspecting officers by six at a time, seemed proud of the attention paid them.

Having made twenty miles the first day, I halted in the evening. My curry and coffee were prepared for me, and, as I felt fatigued, I rested to have a good sleep, and at two in the morning again proceeded on my journey. The next morning being very wet and stormy, I deferred proceeding until the weather moderated, and my servants were not sorry for the delay, as it saved them from exposure to the storm. I had hired eight bearers to accompany me for the whole journey, four bearing me at a time, relieving each other in succession. I found this a good arrangement, as there was no unnecessary delay on the road, though it is more expensive than in laying a regular dâk from the villages on your way, as it is now always arranged in Hindostan. Indeed, I do not think that this country, at the time I am writing of, had regular post-bearers, and I could not have been able to lay them. My palkee was placed under shelter in an old house by the roadside, where my servants could cook and repose themselves.

As the weather on the second morning was still inclement, I delayed my departure, and, as

I could sleep no longer, I raised my pillows to get a volume of Walter Scott from beneath them, to read till breakfast was ready, when I felt something moving under my hand. It occurred instantly to me that a snake might have thought fit to make itself my companion in this weather, as it sometimes does, even in one's bed, to get warm and comfortable. I gently put down my pillows, remaining some short time quiet, as a slight moving of something inside was quite perceptible; but as it is well known to be the best way to lie still in such cases, I did so.

The only difficulty now was to get out without disturbing my friend, whatever it might be. At length, I quietly got free from the covering around me, and, as I did so, saw the scales of a large snake underneath. I, however, got out safely, and proceeded to wake up my servants, who lay muffled up, sleeping around me. In doing so some noise was made, when one of them drew my attention to the head of a very large cobra-capella, reared above my pillows in the palkee, with his hood expanded ready for assault, the noise made in awakening the servants having evidently disturbed his slumbers.

All were very soon on the alert, and sticks used to eject the intruder, but it was not so

easily done. He stuck to his cover, snapping
at the sticks ; at length, a blow on the head
stunned him, when he was thrown out and despatched. He was full five feet in length, and
how such a big fellow could have entered the
palenkeen was a wonder, as only one of the
doors was open a little all night, to admit air,
and the circumference of the snake was over
five inches.

Now, many people, living in ease at home,
may think such occurrences as this are frequent, and that snakes and other noxious reptiles are ever ready to attack you. It is not
so, however ; they will always get out of your
way, if they can, unless you attack them first,
when they will bite or sting you in return.
What I have just mentioned is, with some other
cases of this sort, but seldom met with, and
then not, apparently, with any hostile intention
on the part of the reptiles.

The day cleared up so much after the adventure with the snake, that I was able to have a
walk towards noon, and espied a large piece of
water at some distance, with numerous birds
flying about it. Having my double-barrelled
always ready, I sallied out, and in something
more than an hour returned with three pairs of
whistling teal, so called from the strange whist-

ling noise they make to each other when disturbed. They are nearly the size of a common
duck, and very good eating. With these I
returned, giving them, except one, which I
had roasted for my dinner, to the servants, who
made the usual curries of them.

After dinner the weather became so fine that
I pursued my journey for upwards of twenty-
six miles before halting to refresh the bearers
and give time for the servants to join us.
After ten hours' rest, we again started, and so
continued our route, halting occasionally, and
then off again; and in this way we continued
onwards, occasionally crossing rivers, streams,
and hills, without accident of any kind on our
way for a couple of weeks, until we came in
sight of the Sutlej—our destination, where we
rested some days. Now came the point, how
was I to proceed? when my head man told me
that the bearers would take me to my old
quarters, Simla, at a moderate charge. This
was quite pleasing, for not only should I see that
place and my old friends again, but it relieved
my mind from any anxiety in the matter as to
how I was to proceed farther on my journey, as
I knew that at Simla I could procure ample
means to proceed, either on horseback or by dâk.
On my way to the Plains, I amused myself as

well as I could, sauntering along the banks of
the Sutlej, occasionally gun in hand, for a shot
at waterfowl, which here were scarce.   However, I did rather better with my rod and flies ;
and on one day, after a heavy shower of rain, I
succeeded in catching a good dish of a shining,
or rather silvery-coloured fish, of herring size
and shape, but of deeper body.   They rose
freely at some of my gaudy flies, giving me
much sport.   I cannot say that, in dressing
some of them in our way, their flavour was the
best ; but they made a good curry, and there
was plenty for all, which was a pleasant variety
in our every-day bill of fare.

Having sufficiently rested, we again moved
on, enjoying the fair, cool weather of September, and soon reached the beautiful line of hills
around our destination, on approaching which
I despatched a bearer, on my last day's journey,
with a note to my friend before mentioned,
who had treated me so kindly, and who, I
hoped, was still at Simla.   Nor was I disappointed : he was at home, and no sooner
received my note than he came to join me on
the road, in order to invite me to share the
hospitality of his house, where I found, as
before, everything I could wish.

At breakfast, the news of the day was related

to me, and then the every-day talk of the
station. Some friends were still there, and
were well; others had separated to follow their
duties at their respective posts. There were
a few incidents of a romantic character that
ended in marriage amongst the young folk,
and one or two occurrences of a painful kind,
which sometimes happen at large stations in
India. Some account of my adventures in the
Punjaub seemed to cause much amusement as
well as interest to my friend and his amiable
sister, who were very desirous to know the
feelings of the renowned chief, Runjeet Singh,
towards the English. I related all I had seen
and known regarding his Highness, and his
very friendly feeling for the English nation,
saying that I thought, if we had, as was even
at that time rumoured, any war in the direction
of Afghanistan, that Runjeet Singh would
either be our ally, or remain neutral, in any
conflict that might take place; which, when
it did occur, a couple of years afterwards,
actually proved true.

In the course of the day, my arrival from
Lahore was talked about everywhere, and I
speedily got invitations, not only from former
friends, but from others, greedy to hear the
news of what I had gone through. In due

course I attended their dinner-parties, and had
to relate over again the different scenes I witnessed.   The ladies were particularly anxious
to know what knowledge I had acquired regarding the fairer portion of the Punjaubees,
but on this subject I failed in giving them the
necessary information, although some of them
appeared to find out that I could tell more on
this subject than I was willing to do.

This was to a certain extent true, for
although the Sikh people are more liberal in
their ideas regarding their females than the
same class of persons appear to be in other
parts of the East, still they are by no means
ready to introduce their wives or daughters to
any intercourse or to the observation of other
men; and my knowledge of them generally
was so rare that I could not be a competent
judge, excepting in one or two cases of a most
confidential nature, such as my favoured interview with the beautiful Georgian, to whom I
have before alluded; and in another, when a
well-known chieftain had introduced me to his
wife and children.   The particulars or names
of those parties I did not choose to relate.

In this agreeable way I passed the few days
I intended to remain in this delightful place
before leaving it, perhaps for ever; and having

decided to ride on horseback down the hills, and thence to my old regiment, the Camero- nians, at Meerut, about forty miles distant from them, I bought a nice little half-caste, or rather half-bred, bay Arab, and otherwise prepared for my solitary march to the Plains. The day came, as it always does, when I once more bade farewell to my ever-kind friends; and parting with my servants (who wished to remain with me), except one to attend myself, and another my horse, I proceeded to descend the same road back which I came by, now and then meeting an English traveller, which was a relief, as we always had a talk on the passing events of the day.

In this way I gradually made the principal stations on my way down, to the last on the hills, Subathoo, bordering the kingdom of Nepaul, now governed by its well-known chief, Jung Behauder. This State I wished much to see, and its hardy little Ghoorka soldiers—in- trepid men, particularly in their native hills,— but I had now not sufficient time to do so.

There happened to be a corps of Ghoorkas at that time in our service stationed here, the commandant of which, an English officer, I knew in other days very well, and called upon him. He begged me to remain with him a few days, in remembrance of old times, and dispel the *ennui* he began to feel in having had nobody to associate with for the last six months but his adjutant, and nothing to occupy his time but the routine duties and drill of his corps. My friend being a very well-informed man, I gladly accepted his kind invite. We had many hours of mutual converse, and, amongst other matters, he stated that he had known a good deal of Nepaul and its government, and of the character of its ruler, Jung Behauder, who had got into power by what we should justly call unlawful means. Still, he had afterwards, by his courage, firmness, and good management, put down the discord and disturbances that prevailed over the country at that time, and had ever since governed it so well that the country was in a most prosperous state, and my friend believed him to be a firm ally of England. In my stories to him, relative to all that happened to me, he was much interested, particularly as regarded the last country I had visited, and its friendly feeling towards us.

In this way time flew happily away, and few except those who have experienced it can conceive how pleasing to the mind is the meeting of old friends, long separated in foreign lands. We varied our amusements by

giving a day to shooting, in which we bagged
some of the common brown pheasant and a
couple of pea-fowl, which were duly consigned
to an excellent cook, the former to be roasted,
and some curried—the latter to produce that
famous Eastern soup, called mulkautani.

Having stated to my friend a wish I had to
see his Ghoorkas before leaving, he at once consented, and had them paraded accordingly, the
day before my departure. On that day there
assembled two hundred and fifty well-appointed
active little men, in green rifle dress, who
formed column and marched past in quick
time, with arms advanced, sloping, and carried,
as a salute, in passing us, very well indeed;
then they changed front from line in skir-
mishing order, and I must say that I thought
better or more active soldiers for this important
duty could not well be found. The whole corps,
with a reserve, then formed an advanced guard
in the woods around, and I never saw it better
done, or so quickly. Their fire was well timed
and well sustained, and they showed themselves
the very men for it, particularly in this mountainous and deeply-wooded country. All this
occupied about a couple of hours, when they
formed, marched past as before, and then dis-
missed, after having been most justly praised

for their performance in the field, as well as for their good conduct at all times, with which the men appeared highly pleased. The dinner of this day was highly relished—it was excellent. In taking leave afterwards the moment was saddened by the word farewell; however, this must be so always in this world, either for good or evil.

Next morning at daylight I mounted my horse, when my friend met and accompanied me for a couple of miles on my road. We then again bade adieu, and sorry I was to hear it was the last, as he, unfortunately for his friends and the service, died a few months after, of jungle fever. I seldom met with a more agreeable companion.

In resuming my way down, the sun broke out lovely to behold, throwing a brightness and beauty on the scene shortly before darkened by heavy clouds. There lay the vast and rich plains before me, spread out as on a map, far as the eye could reach; and around me were the still beautiful and varied hills, sloping off and diminishing in height as they approached the low grounds. The palm-tree, the pine, and the rhododendron appeared dwarfed in comparison to those I left behind. The shrubs and flowers, too, were much less in size; but there

N

were still in the valleys the cyprus and myrtle, the latter as beautiful and sweet-smelling as ever. Sprinkled about were many pretty bungalows, surrounded by their well laid-out gardens, owned by many whose occupations were here locally situated, or belonging to gentlemen on their respective duties elsewhere. The whole presented a landscape of much domestic beauty, heightened by the sight of a number of rivulets meandering through the valleys, and a variety of small birds, mostly fly-catchers, arrayed in varied and rich plumage, flitting along the rivulets in search of their daily food.

I was now leaving behind me all that was so strikingly lovely in scenery, and, like the last rose of summer, fading away, as I descended lower and lower, until at length the travellers' bungalow came in sight, at the foot of the hills. Here I found, after all, something to comfort me, in the shape of a roasted pheasant and a curry, which my servant, having started before me, had ready prepared for me.

It is fortunate for erring man that in his most sublime moments, his appetite, if good, gets the better of his feelings; and so much was it so in my case, that I nearly finished the pheasant, and the curry too, with infinite good-will, leaving my poor servant so small an allowance of the last dish, that I think he said, in consequence of my preferring this low country air to the mountain, "Yes, it is very good for master: he come down hill—his appetite come plenty better."

He made me laugh, and I then gave him my last pheasant to make for himself a plentiful curry. This he had ready in half an hour, for in making this dish they never pluck a fowl, but dip him, feathers and all, in hot water. He is then instantly skinned, broken up, and ready for use.

Having finished my claret and coffee, after a walk in the neighbourhood, I retired to my cot, sleeping soundly until nearly four o'clock next morning, generally my time of rising.

A few quiet marches would take me to Meerut, where my late regiment still was, and where I intended to remain some days. I accordingly pursued my way, without incident of any kind, over the uninteresting plains, until again the far-famed Delhi broke upon my sight. On passing through it everything appeared as I had left it, and I put up outside, at the usual bungalow for travellers.

As my last march brought me in sight of Meerut, I perceived, as the sun peeped out across the horizon, a red line on the parade-

ground, and soon made it out to be the Came-
ronians, returning to their barracks after their
morning march, with their gallant colonel at
their head—Colonel Oglander, who once every
week marched his men in line for about three
miles, then right about face and back again, in
the same order; and nothing could be finer or
better done than this simple, but difficult move-
ment to maintain correctly; and certainly this
fine regiment, nearly a thousand bayonets, did
it to perfection.

I was made an honorary member of the mess
the instant it was known that I had come, and
duly attended that evening; and when I arrived
the pipes were blowing away merrily for dinner.
The table was spread, and amongst other good
things was a haggis, deliciously made, with the
fresh spices of the East mixed in it to perfection.   After all had done justice to the goodly
fare, we adjourned to the smoking-room, where
my old messmates said, " Come, Nevill, have a
meerschaum, then we'll have a bowl of whisky
toddy, when we know you will sing us, ' Scots
wha ha' wi' Wallace bled !' then ' Over the hills
and far away !' and then to bed till morning
dawns.''

It was thus I passed a most delightful evening.
Many years have gone away since then; but

often busy memory recalls the past charming phases of my life, and brings a smile to its recollection.

The second evening came and went in the same pleasing manner, during which some sitting near me said, " You know how glad we are to see you, and we don't think there can be any mistake about that; so do pray let us hear something regarding what you have seen in the land of the Sikh." I willingly complied, and full attention was paid to my tale throughout.

A grand ceremony was now announced as about to take place, which was to be followed by a banquet at Sirdahna, near which town was the palace of her Highness the celebrated Begum Sumroo, to which the officers of the regiment were invited, including myself.

This princess had conformed to the Catholic faith, and a celebration in her Highness's chapel* was to take place by a dignitary of that Church, well known as Monsignore Julius Cæsar, who, at our mess, sometimes sang of the glory of Nelson and the battle of the Nile, with considerable effect.

The day arrived, and a procession was formed of the converts to the Christian faith. Some of these had been admitted to the priesthood, and

* In honour of a saint.

were dressed in white surplices, having silver incense vases in their hands, waving about, sending forth clouds of rich perfume. The procession, as usual, was headed by bearers with gilt crosses.

Then came the bishop, in his mitre and splendid blue velvet robes, covered with embroidered crosses. After him came a sort of litter of crimson velvet, gorgeously gilded, in which was seated her Highness, attended by her relative, Colonel Dyce Sombre,* commanding the troops of the princess, and other officers of the State.

Her Highness, though seventy-five years of age, was yet good-looking and attractive; and as I bowed to her, in passing, I thought of the many varied scenes of her past adventurous career—memorable from so many vicissitudes of fortune, that a book might be written on the remarkable events connected with her past life.

The doors were now thrown open, and the procession proceeded along the elegant mosaic-paved aisle, chaunting psalms in Latin, to the High Altar, of great beauty, in a blaze of light. The ceremony was gone through with much dignity, and then the bishop blessed the

* A very kind and very clever man.

princess; and as her Highness raised her hands in prayer, her arms became uncovered—white, and still beautiful. Her Highness, though of small stature, must have been once eminently handsome.

High Mass was celebrated with good music, and the exquisitely rich voice of an Italian clergyman and others. So this impressive ceremony closed, and it is difficult to describe the grandeur of the scene, together with the brilliancy of the sun, sparkling through the painted windows. No words can tell their effect upon the beholder, blended with tints of softened hues around you, in this very pretty chapel, such as we never see at home.

Feelings quiet and mysterious stole over me as I left this most interesting place; but I was soon awakened from Fancy's dream by the guns of her Highness firing a salute in honour of the occasion, which brought my mind back again to every-day life.

All the officers attending the ceremony had apartments in the palace, and anything wanted, and called for by them, was instantly complied with.

Any one who has been in the East can understand the magnificence of fireworks there displayed on important occasions; and their appearance this night, I think, surpassed in splendour anything I had ever seen before. In our cold, moist climate the fireworks we exhibit are but tame and dull in comparison.

The banquet followed the fireworks, and was laid in the grand saloon of the palace.* This room, at least a hundred feet long, and nearly as many broad, was throughout encased with Chunam polished marble, and enriched with flowers on the walls, and other ornaments in lapis-lazuli of varied colours, all rich, and first-rate in effect.

There were three tables, ranged alongside each other, covered with cloths of superb damask, on which were placed every luxury that either the East or the West could furnish. On a raised dais, covered by a golden canopy, sat the princess, dressed in white muslin robes, with a chain of large pearls round her neck, which held a large diamond cross of great value. Round her Highness, sitting on cushions, below her, were some handsome damsels, her attendants. Those ladies had apparently conformed to her Highness's new faith, for they all wore rich crosses on their necks. On a marble table by her side stood a small hookah, a costly-looking article, the jewelled pipe of

* Mostly in ruins at the Mutiny, 1857.

which the princess lowered to her side with much grace as her guests came forward to pay their respects in succession.

We then sat down to the feast, and after the first course, Colonel Dyce Sombre* announced that it was the wish of her Highness that we should charge our glasses. The health of William IV. of England was then drunk, all standing. This was followed by the health of her Highness the Begum Sumroo, who then rose, and, bowing courteously around, retired, attended by her suite.

We then right earnestly began to enjoy ourselves, the good cheer and fine wine having their effect upon us in producing much wit and repartee of a happy kind. After some time, those who could sing well were called upon, as was customary with us in those days, far away from home. As the evening advanced, we broke up, some for home, others to play at cards or billiards, a few to see the celebrated company of the Almæ dance; and thus terminated this superb banquet.

* On the death of the Begum Sumroo, this gentleman went to England with a very large fortune, and married Lord St. Vincent's daughter.

CHAPTER IX.

1835.

HAVING remained long enough in Meerut, I hired a budgerow to convey me down the mighty Ganges—or, as often called, the Hoogly—to Cawnpore, and eventually to Calcutta. This budgerow (I suppose now well known) is a broad native boat, constructed so as to admit of a bungalow, generally of bamboo and matting. There were two apartments, and a stable for my horse.

The prow of this boat is sometimes adorned with an idol, or hideous figure-head, having no bowsprit; the only sails in common use, according to its size, are either one, two, or three lug-sails, hoisted one above another in the fashion of square-rigged vessels. These boats generally sail very well, offering little resistance to the water; but they very often upset when sailing in a strong wind, being for the most part top-heavy.

The manji, or master of the boat, directs the helm: another man stands in the bows, with a long bamboo, to shove off from all

banks, rocks, and other obstructions. There
were six other men, three of a side, with most
primitive paddles, with which they aided in
propelling the boat; and so we proceeded at
a quick rate, and in fine weather it is a very
pleasant mode of travelling. Here you have
leisure and opportunity to contemplate the fine
views and towns on your way, and particularly
the numerous temples of various creeds, all
unique, and marked by beauty : indeed, the
scenery in many parts of the river is highly
picturesque, and furnishes your sketch-book
with very beautiful examples of form and
colouring, light and shade.

The charming appearance of the slender
minarets and clustering domes of the mosque,
rising one above another, of the moslem,
together with the more massive-built pagodas
of the Hindoo with their quaint decorations,
and the very queer jumble of native villages
and streets, form a whole so novel to the sight,
and often so striking, that I defy the beholder,
be he ever so lazy, to pass them without trans-
ferring their appearance to his sketch-book.
You thus, aided by reading, pass your time
most agreeably.

When evening came, I had either a walk or,
when practicable, landed my horse, and had

a scamper along the shore. The banks, however, of a shifting nature, are very treacherous,
and sometimes, when walked on, they sink
with yourself into the river. I have in this
way got a sound ducking. In case a storm
should arise, it is absolutely necessary to pull
up the boat and anchor off a protecting bank.

Wild-fowl, partridge, hare, and larger animals are met with on the shore, and, for the
sportsman going down, prove an addition to
his dinner. Nor are fish to be forgotten, nor
the alligator, certain parts of which a native
considers good food.

I happened to get close to a young one,
about three feet long, on which I poured, at
about ten yards' distance, such a potent charge
of shot, that he hardly stirred, only kicking
a bit; and an hour afterwards he was bubbling
in the pots of my attendants.

I occasionally caught some good fish with
my rod and flies, catching sometimes the delicate tupsi and other smaller fish; and, once in
a way, one which very much resembled the
pomfret, but larger than I have seen it taken
on the Madras coast. The curry made by this
fellow was excellent.

One day I put on a salmon-fly: a dash was
soon made at it by a large fish; but I lost

him, and the fly too. Seeing some large fish in shallow water, I twisted a piece of bright tin, above a large hook, to which I attached a strong line, to act as a spinner under water; but I paid for this experiment by having my rod broken. A mahsir of large size took it, at the same time bouncing above water, showing his dimensions, something like four feet, and thick in proportion. One of the boatmen jumped overboard, and caught the broken piece of rod and line; but the fish broke the line in a moment, and got out of his reach.

While this was going on, a huge mugger* raised himself close to the boatman, who became frightened, and dashed off to the shore. We all shouted to frighten the monster, who evidently appeared to look after the fish, splashing about, entangled in the piece of line and rod, and no doubt swallowed him, as we lost sight of both shortly after. The man, after a good deal of trouble, we got on board again, more dead than alive.

There are some people who have a great dislike to eat fish caught in the Ganges: I have no such feeling. It perhaps will not prove pleasant to know what our own fish feed on

* Broad-nosed alligator. Some of these monsters are from twenty-five to thirty feet in length.

sometimes. No doubt it is disagreeable to think that dead bodies are every day consigned to the waters of the Sacred Ganges; but then we are not always to take it for granted that they are eaten by the fish.

We had generally fine weather, and got on very well; but in sailing round curves of the river, there is sometimes much difficulty experienced in avoiding collision with boats wending their way up the stream. These latter boats being pulled, by means of ropes fastened to their bows, by " trackers," or men either on shore or wading in shallow water, cannot well get out of the way of those coming down, and therefore a good deal depends upon skill in steering to avoid accident.

On one occasion we struck the bow of a budgerow coming up. Both boats were all but upset; fortunately, our sails went over the side on the crash taking place. The coming boat got the worst of it, as her bows were much injured. And never did I hear such an uproar as it occasioned on board both boats, one accusing the other of stupidity in the matter; and I must say the natives of the East are by no means deficient in using ugly language, when angry, towards each other, any more than their brethren of the West, whom they beat hollow in words of abuse. In the other boat were some women and children, and the screaming of these was fearful. " We shall all go to the bottom, and be eaten by the alligators," was one of their exclamations. After all this terror, there was not so much harm done. We managed to get the boats on shore to repair damages, and some rupees from me reconciled matters. After three days' hammering and splicing, we were again both ready for a start. It often happens, in bad weather, that boats are sunk, either by collision or sandbanks, and some lives lost. We parted good friends the fourth day after the accident, and our boat proceeded in the usual way for some weeks on our route to Cawnpore, my time being employed in reading, sketching, shooting, &c.

One day we passed an immense swampy piece of ground, swarming with wild geese. They occasionally got up in such dense masses, that I fired at them with ball, occasionally bringing one down ; but such was the impracticable nature of the ground, that it was impossible to get them.

Three days before we reached our destination, we had the good fortune to weather a fearful storm. It was foretold by the approach of heavy masses of dark clouds surrounding us, and a deep moaning noise of wind. The manji said we must lose no time in securing the boat. We made for a deep nook on the left bank of the river, in which we secured her, taking in sails, masts, &c. The storm began, a wild commotion whirled vapour about us in all directions, then burst upon us a dire tornado, which laid prostrate everything exposed to its influence. The high palm-trees in the plain were bowed to the earth; the plantain, the vine, and other trees and shrubs were strewed in fragments everywhere.* The vivid lightning hissed around, and the rattling thunder shook from the black revolving clouds a storm of hail almost as terrible as that which is described by Moses as having fallen upon the Egyptians. The hailstones were so large that, in striking, they cut the face or hands severely.

It was most fortunate for us that we were so well protected on either side by two sound, high banks, else our frail bungalow, boat and all, I think, must have gone. My little horse trembled in every limb, and broke out in profuse perspira-

---

* A fine old banyan-tree stood it out better than any of the rest. This tree is well known from the extent to which it grows; stems descending from the branches to the ground, take root, and extend *ad infinitum.*

tion. Nor did he altogether get off clear. One
of the boatmen, securing a rope to the side of
the vessel, was struck by the lightning, and,
poor fellow, blinded for ever. He received
no other injury, however. This dreadful weather
lasted nearly three hours, and then gradually
cleared away, to our inexpressible delight.

When we were able to look around, we beheld
a wild and desolate sight. Far as the eye
could reach, the ground was covered with hailstones, fallen trees, and fragments of all kinds.
On the evening of this eventful day, I was
rather surprised to find the manji and his men
busy in getting the boat out of the creek which
so well protected us during the storm. The
river, too, was very much swollen, and hereabouts abounded in sandbanks of a shifting
nature. On inquiry, I heard that the reason
for moving away from the left bank of the river
to the right was, that on the right bank we
were on British territory, and comparatively
safe from robbers attacking us; whereas, where
we then were, was on the borders of the King
of Oude's territories; and that plundering-
parties belonging to that State were ever on
the look-out for boats meeting with accidents,
lurking on the banks, ready to take advantage of any mishap that might happen to

o

travellers,* and after the storm were sure to be out watching.

I had hardly heard this, when two horsemen, well armed, appeared, galloping alongside the river. They suddenly stopped, and looked towards us; and as we were disengaging the vessel from the shore, one head popped up before us, then another. A matchlock was pointed at the boat, and the owner of the matchlock said, " You must wait until we see who you are." The manji, coming to me, said, " Sir, master put on his uniform, and show himself; they will not attack us, as they are very much afraid of English officer." (I was then dressed something in the native way.) I lost no time in doing so; but, before I was quite ready, I heard a shot, followed by some of the boatmen rushing on me. I had then my uniform-coat on, and dashed out to the side of the boat, pistols in hand, just in time, as some of the rascals were coming on board. On seeing me, as I shouted to them in English, about a dozen of them scampered off in every direction, which I was really not sorry for, and, as an adieu, fired amongst them, but did not see that my ball had taken effect. We had no

* Whom they plundered, and afterwards usually murdered.

further annoyance, and at length got the vessel
well into the river, when on she went at a great
rate; but there was little or no wind, and
before it was quite dark we anchored on our
side of the river all right.

As the dâk, or post, was to pass near us next
morning, I prepared a note for my old friend
and comrade, George Mansel, then captain in
the 16th Lancers, stationed at Cawnpore. We
had both lived together and hunted together
for some years, when in the 30th Infantry,
serving in the Deccan. He was a very excellent
fellow—nothing appeared to put him out of
temper—and one of the boldest sportsmen I
ever met with. We were one day out shooting,
and I separated from him in pursuit of a peafowl, which led me a long way to get it: when
I fell in with him again, he was surrounded by
natives. Inside the circle was himself, and
beside him a dead panther. This panther had
slaughtered several sheep, and had made such
a hearty meal of some of them, that he lay
down near his victims, in some bushes. The
natives, on seeing Mansel approach the place,
prayed of him to kill their enemy, pointing out
the spot where it was. Without a moment's
hesitation, he mounted his horse, gun in hand,
and charged at the panther, who thought it

best, on this occasion, to make off. Mansel followed him, and, when within a few yards, discharged both barrels into his side, killing him, fortunately, on the spot. The brute was gorged, certainly, and could neither spring well nor run fast ; but this does not take off from the courage shown in the matter. The panther, when enraged or hungry, is most ferocious, and will attack anything.

We kept a strict watch during the night, but were not disturbed. Next morning I despatched my note. We then proceeded on our way, and, without further interruption, reached the principal ghât of Cawnpore. The first person I saw there was Mansel, and I think he was as glad to see me as I him. My horse and baggage being landed and despatched to his house, we proceeded together to his hospitable home, where we were welcomed by the lady, his wife, who greeted me well on my return from the interior of the East. Here I lived for some weeks, enjoying his society, always accompanying him to his field-duties and to stables, and passing my time most agreeably.

The 16th Lancers, a distinguished regiment, were in their full strength, and presented a magnificent appearance in their very handsome dress and black plumes. They were com-

manded by one of the finest fellows in the
army, the celebrated Colonel Arnold. He
accompanied his regiment on the expedition to
Afghanistan, and died of fatigue at Cabul. It
was too much for him. He was an old Peninsular soldier, and I knew him at the terrible
storm of Badajoz, then as a young officer in the
4th Infantry, where he was wounded.

Cawnpore, at this time a celebrated place on
this side of India, was the principal station
both for a large military force and as a resort
of the Civil Service, who, with their ladies,
made the place very gay. The military there,
besides the Lancers, were the 16th British
Infantry, a large body of artillery, and several
native regiments, of both cavalry and infantry.

At this season (October, 1835), it was cool
and refreshing, and many people came here on
a visit to their friends, to pass an agreeable
time; but Cawnpore, for at least six months
in the year, is anything but a desirable place:
the heat during the so-called summer months
is terrible, accompanied by whirlwinds of
fine sand from the plain; every house is
shut up during the day, and double windows, custus tatties, and puncas kept constantly going day and night, in order to cool
down the heated atmosphere. In this and

other respects Meerut is a far more eligible residence, and is so near the Himalayas that an invalid, in thirty hours or so, by dâk, reaches them, and a fine climate, to rescue him from the oppression of the hot months.

It was the intention of the officers of the 16th Lancers to celebrate the anniversary of a battle in which they played a stirring part, by a grand ball, and to keep it on for three days— that is, during that time to provide for their guests breakfast, dinner, supper, &c.—and prepared for it accordingly; and no expense was spared in the furnishing and decoration of some acres of ground round their mess-house. This they inclosed by kurnauts, or screens, in the interior of which were marquees pitched, and provided with every luxury possible.

The appointed time arrived. All the officers of the force and their ladies, together with all the others, ladies and gentlemen, at the station, were present, as well as all the princes and native chiefs around; and when I entered, a magnificent sight presented itself: the dazzling beauty of the scene, the splendid uniforms—for all were in full dress—were unexampled. Here was Scindia, the head of the Mahratta kingdom, dressed in cloth-of-gold covered with precious stones; the Maharajah Holkar, the Peishwar,

and numerous other native dignitaries, all re-
splendent in dress and jewellery.   Here was
also, as he was then called, his Highness the
Nana Sahib, a powerful-looking man, but I
thought there was something sinister and for-
bidding in his face.   He was noted, both here
and at Meerut, for giving grand entertainments
to British officers.

In the sets for dancing there was a good
sprinkling of beautiful women, and amongst
them was 'Miss Churchill, well known for her
wit and attractive manners, daughter of Colonel
Churchill, killed afterwards at Mahrajhpore.
This fairy-like fête was spiritedly carried out
by Colonel Arnold and his officers, and during
the three days it lasted nothing was wanting to
make it desirable to remain and to enjoy.

In thinking upon the reminiscences I have
written regarding other days, I am reminded
of the great changes that have taken place in
India since then, in the last twenty years and
upwards, and the principal cause or causes
of the dreaful mutiny of the sepoys and natives
against our authority in 1857.   First, then,
was, that the native princes and chiefs were,
secretly, always against us.   The sepoys, next,
were jealous of us, and were indifferently
officered and disciplined (with many excep-

tions*) in this part of India, compared with the Bombay or Madras Presidencies.

When we conquered Scinde and the Punjaub, we very unwisely either sent Europeans on to occupy the conquered countries, or withdrew the force that garrisoned Cawnpore and Meerut. This was taken advantage of by the native chiefs, and conspiracies were formed long before the explosion took place, which ended with great loss of both men and money on our side, and the destruction of hundreds of defenceless women and children.† Every one who has served in India must know the danger of leaving the country denuded of European troops, and therefore to have done so in this combustible part of India was inexcusable at that time.

On the termination of this grand fête, I prepared for my journey; and having now but little use for my horse, I gave him to Mansel, with whom I knew he would be well cared for. And then the parting adieu took place, an

* The European Bengal Artillery were amongst the best I ever saw, particularly the Horse Artillery, which were unrivalled.

† When before the enemy with my regiment, my native servant told me he had seen spies in the camp, who had been counting the Europeans present; they did not mind the native force.

event which, in some cases, is particularly distressing amongst soldiers, who, from the nature
of their duties and the casualties they are
subject to, so often part to meet no more.

In pursuing our journey downwards, we still
bordered the States of Oude, and I had some
good shooting, occasionally, at hogs, which
I found in great plenty.   They are capital
eating, especially when their food is vegetable,
bulbs and roots procured from the soil they
frequent.

Without any event taking place worthy of
notice, we made our way to Allahabad, upwards
of two hundred miles from Cawnpore.   This is
considered by the Hindoos to be a very holy
place, from the point of confluence of the
Jumna and the Ganges being here.   There is
seen a distinct line of colour between the two
rivers as they glide down together, the one being
distinguishable as clear and bluish, the other a
yellowish brown ; and so they flow on together
for a very considerable distance before appearing to mix their waters.   The Hindoos
come from very distant places to bathe here ;
and in those waters they believe, not only that
their bodies are to be healed of any disease
they may be subject to, but that their souls also
become purified from sin.

On the headland between the two rivers stands a fort remarkable for its impressive appearance. It is partly modern in its structure outside, having a land-front of fortification on Vauban's system, erected in other days by the French, the entrance to which is by a very handsome gateway in the Grecian style of architecture. In the inside is rather a confused jumble of temples, tombs, &c., in the usual lofty and massive style of the Hindoos. The town is large, irregular, and very dirty.

All around, on the banks of the river, presents a singular spectacle; hundreds of pilgrims are seen, going through different forms of ablution and prayer. They at times perform all sorts of absurd antics and ceremonies, flinging themselves about without much regard to prudence or delicacy. Many barbers were running here and there to shave men's heads before bathing, as they believe here that the more the head is shaved, the nearer they are to the joys of paradise, in case of death within a certain time.

Pursuing my course down the Ganges, I found we got on much more rapidly than higher up. The tide began to have influence, so that, when we had in our favour both wind and tide, the sailing was pleasing, and the deeper waters rendered less the fear of running on sand-banks. Porpoises from the sea sometimes appeared, and enormous alligators showed themselves, and often had a shot from me. Numerous dead bodies were seen floating down in all manner of shapes, totally nude, as they always are when consigned to the care of this sacred river; and we soon got to the far-famed sacred city of Benares, about one hundred and fifty miles from Allahabad. Here I was re-solved to remain for some days; but, before attempting to describe the interior of the place, I must say something of the marvellous beauty of the scene on our approach to it.*

The day was closing when, in winding down the river, the Holy City of Benares burst full upon my sight; and never did I behold any place erected by the hands of man so im-pressive. It blended well with the enchanting scenery around, and, illuminated by the golden tints of the setting sun, was reflected by the great river as in a plateau of molten silver.

Benares is built upon the acclivity of a high sloping bank, spreading over the crest towards

* Bacon's "Hindostan" gives an excellent description of this side of India. His sketches illustrating the scenery are truly beautiful.

the level country. The greater number of the buildings are temples and religious edifices, and the water's edge is a continued line of ghâts, and very handsome, wide stone steps, in various styles of architecture, the designs being almost as different as those of the temples.

Throughout the whole of this vast Hindoo city, I do not think two temples or two ghâts will be found in the same fashion of architecture. They are piled up, one above the other, in most elaborate but imposing confusion; being beautifully decorated, and some fancifully coloured.

All these buildings belong to the Hindoos, with one exception, and that is a grand one, which attracts immediate notice. It is a large mosque for Moslem worship, the only one in the city, with two beautiful slender minarets of great height, standing above the Hindoo temples with a proud air of superiority. This mosque was built by the famed Aurungzebe, after his capture of Benares, the representative of whom, now shorn of his glory and title of emperor, is the Nizam of Hydrabad.

The population of Benares is said to be something near eight thousand souls, a small number of whom are Mahomedans. Some of the native merchants are very wealthy, and

I beheld many shops containing manufactures apparently of immense value : cloths woven with gold and silver, beautiful muslins embroidered with the same, besides fringes and ornaments of every kind.

Hindoo mythology is better known and more studied here than it is in any other part of India ; but for an Englishman, however learned he may be, to give a correct history of the multitude of idols representing Hindoo worship, is, I really think, impossible.

Some of the figures displayed in the temples forcibly reminded me of those I saw in Assyria and Egypt : for instance, several idols, bullheaded ; others bearing the front of an elephant upon the shoulders of a man, winged figures upon limbs of men, and horses. Some are to be seen in the mighty caves of Ellora, at Aurungabad (caves and idols hewn out of the solid rock) ; several here are of a black colour, with great extended wings, like a huge bat. In one temple is seen, beautifully carved, a chariot drawn by a horse with six heads. In another temple was a most frightful idol, with something like the face of a man, having several arms encircled, with armlets of serpents. In another temple were seen women performing menial offices to the idol therein worshipped.

And there were figures of both sexes in other temples, of a most profane character ; but few I was allowed to visit, and those few, with their idols, were mostly all incarnations of the powers of Brahma, the Great Eternal, showing his attributes through Vishnu, the saving, and Siva, the destroying power of his creation.

Here the sacred books of Shasters of the Hindoos were, day and night, read aloud in the temples, and sometimes were beautifully sung and intoned. All the menial offices of the Brahmin priests were performed by women appointed to those temples, who were not allowed to mix with their own sex, or with any one else, out of them. The beautiful Mahomedan mosque I was desirous to visit, but, as it was a feast-time, I was not permitted.

I happened to meet a gentleman of the civil service, in my wandering about, whom I knew, and he told me he was very much perplexed how to act in a case of suttee, or wife-burning with a deceased husband. He knew the parties. The husband was a young landholder of his district, and died suddenly. They were people of high caste, and the young and handsome widow was determined to burn with the man of her choice, nor could any persuasion on

my friend's part prevent it. I was curious to
see this tragedy, and as he was resolved to be
present to the last and urge the widow against
it, I asked and obtained leave to accompany
him at the appointed time.

We followed a crowd of natives surrounding
a hackery, or car, led by Brahmins (all were
highly excited), to the banks of the river, some
way from the city, where the sacrifice was to
take place.*   When they stopped, my friend,
the young judge, descended with me from his
carriage and approached to the inner party,
where I beheld a very beautiful creature
standing — the devoted wife. The judge ex-
horted the lady to withdraw along with him
and her relations, but all in vain. The Brahmins then speedily placed faggots beside the
pile ; the wife took leave of her father, mother,
and friends, giving them all the costly jewels
she wore. She then ascended the pile, placing
herself beside the body of her husband, smiling
as she gazed upon him ; then, taking a burning
faggot from a Brahmin, she, with undaunted
courage, set fire to the pile herself. A dense
mass of smoke and flame arose and hid her from
our sight; in a short time the whole fell inwards,

* A similar case is mentioned in Mr. Coleman's work on
Indian Mythology.

and both living and dead were consumed to ashes. I felt sick, and rather faint, at this dreadful ceremony; and when I returned to the carriage, both the judge and I were much relieved by a small dose of brandy he had ready in his case.

We again continued our voyage, and got to Ghazepore in five days, and had much difficulty in getting out of the way of numerous sand-banks. The windings of the river render the distance from Benares (about forty miles) nearly double.

Ghazepore has ever been celebrated for the growth of its rose-trees. Here are large fields of them, and the sweet flowers are cultivated for the manufacture of rose-water, the scent of which is so very delicious, and its cooling properties such a relief in warm climates. All attempts, however, to consolidate the juice into attar entirely fail, as, on exposure to the air, the attar immediately liquefies. The town, although large, has nothing very striking about it; like most other Indian towns, it is dirty in the interior and narrow in the streets. There are extensive barracks, and sometimes a regiment of Europeans is quartered here.

Ten miles further on we made Dinapore, a

large military station and a flourishing place, as there is a good trade carried on of all kinds, native and European.   The native workmen are very expert in their imitation of any European article: give them but a " muster," as they call it, of what you want made, and the tradesman whose business it is copies it to a nicety.   A shoemaker will stand before you, and either sell you ready-made boots or shoes, or take your measure for the same: if boots, the charge will be two rupees; if shoes, under one.   I here bought twenty pounds of excellent wax candles for less than eight rupees, and all other things are equally cheap.

There were a good number of European gentlemen and ladies residing here, of both civil and military services, and a tolerable sprinkling of fashionable young ladies from home; many of these last being on their way to friends stationed in the Upper Provinces, all eager to see the new comers and the newest fashions from England.

The scenery all along the river from Bhagul-poor to the Rajmahal hills, which bound the horizon, is exceedingly picturesque and beautiful.   The whole district, for hundreds of miles, appears highly cultivated, and is considered the richest land in our possession.

Our every-day life was much the same, and I began to wish very much to get to Calcutta for a change of scene. From what my manji told me regarding the people residing in the hills we were approaching, I resolved, when passing, to land and pay them a temporary visit; and, when the time came, I sallied forth, accompanied by my servant and a couple of boatmen. It was early morning, and therefore, before the sun arose, we got some miles on the hills, in the province of Orissa. Having had our breakfast, we approached one of the villages, and met both men and women perfectly distinct in appearance, manners, and habits from those of the plains we had just left. They speak a different language, which was understood by one of my boatmen, who had for some time resided amongst them, and to whom they said, "We dislike the low-country people so much, that we seldom or never go down to buy anything. The people below, at certain times in the year, visit us with grain or cattle; we pay for whatever we purchase, but there our intercourse ceases."

These people are exceedingly primitive in their habits, and possess also a simplicity of character very remote from the inhabitants of the low countries, being averse to cunning, theft, and lying—the three chief accomplishments of the common classes of black men.

The men, like all highlanders, are muscular, and infinitely finer than any I have seen since my sojourn in the Punjaub. The women are light-coloured, and freely showed themselves to us while conversing. They pay for anything bought by them generally in quantities of delicious honey, some of the hill grain, and charcoal.

Having had our curry under a friendly tree hard by the village, we prepared for our return to the boat as evening closed. Next morning we proceeded, and were carried down this mighty river rapidly, a fine breeze blowing in our favour, until we came to a channel or branch of the Hoogly running into the Ganges, which here expanded in width to nearly three miles; and the appearance of this expanse of water, studded here and there with small islands, or banks covered with verdure, was most striking and picturesque. It is to be remarked that a description of the Ganges and its branches must not be implicitly relied on, as the banks on both sides are continually shifting, so that a village overlooking the water this season may be far distant from it next season, or, *vice versâ*, the remains of it may be in the stream itself.   In cities or large towns close to the river are raised barriers of wood, and earth within well rammed down; but even these, in stormy weather, are broken or forced away—such is the power of the current and the uncertainty of the foundation, exposing the town to inundation.

Rajhmahal, which we passed, is one of the most interesting places, from its antiquity, on the river.   Two hundred years are gone since it was the splendid capital of the Mahomedans on this side of the East.   There are yet to be seen vast and splendid ruins, showing the magnificence of other days.   Interspersed amongst them are stately waving bamboos and other trees, some of large growth; but the gateway of Rajhmahal, still nearly perfect, from its lofty dimensions and singular beauty, is unrivalled.

There exists, in a tract of country to the south-west of the Rajhmahal hills, forming the northern boundary of the province of Orissa, a wild and savage race, called Koles.   The district they inhabit is very desolate and unproductive, parts of it being intersected by deep ravines and watercourses, and overrun with impenetrable jungle.   Its climate is most pestilential, and seldom or never visited even by sportsmen, although it is said to abound in game of all kinds.

There is scarcely any cultivation of the soil, and the inhabitants appear, like the Goands on the hills around Nagpoor, to perform it in the most primitive and uncivilized fashion, the natives being too ignorant and stupid to profit by example, and too superstitious to venture upon any innovation upon their established usages, or to desire improvement of any kind. They are athletic and strong in appearance, of very dark complexion, with coarse lips and savage features, indicating much similarity to some of the African tribes.   In temper they are sullen, tyrannical, and revengeful towards each other, without the restriction of any religion, their nearest approach to it being superstition in its foulest forms; and slaves to a fermented liquor, which they prepare from the cocoanut.   The most revolting part of their savage conduct exists in the indiscriminate marriages, which usually take place between members of the same family, and the total neglect of the other decencies of life, which are so strictly observed by the neighbouring Hindoos, with whom they sometimes come in contact, though only for the purpose of purchasing arrack,* with which they return home, and never cease to drink until they are in a brutal state of intoxication.

They must be the descendants from some savage people, but how or by what means they came to be where they are now located, no record of any kind exists to tell the story. This people are detested by all the other natives of this' side of India, who call them Cafres and infidels of a very bad kind.

It was now December, and as we were progressing satisfactorily towards Calcutta, I certainly felt right glad to be near my long journey's end; still I must give a sort of general description of what was so strikingly beautiful on my passage down the river. We passed many large towns and military stations without stopping. The scenery, of the character which I have before described, was sometimes very fine, at other times with intervening wastes of sandy plains. We had a fair wind and fine weather nearly all the way down; and, to sum up, the very many picturesque views which are to be met with cannot fail to fill one with wonder and delight, and furnish the artist with never-failing examples of ex-

* Distillation from rice.

quisite forms of colouring, and of light and shade. The confused pile of buildings in a native city; the lofty gateways and massive granite walls, with deep mouldings and quaint decorations; the broad ghâts, or flights of steps, from the water to the temples, in every form of Eastern architecture, skirted by the low dingy habitations of the poorer classes, have a grotesque but wonderfully imposing air, and present an extraordinary combination of the grand and elegant, together with that which is mean and unsightly.

Again, the banks afford exquisite little specimens of the beautiful in a more simple and homely character. The ruined tomb, or the peasant's mud hut, sheltered by an overhanging tamarind-tree or the matted banyan, is thrown into quiet repose by the coolness of the shadow opposing the warm evening lights.

To all these local beauties add the graceful palm and lofty cocoanut, the thickly-clustered pepul, the feathery jhynt, and spreading mango, which lend a peculiar grace, quite novel to the eye of the new comer. Then, again, may be seen the broad undulating plain, or wide expanse of lake, lit up with the vivid accidental lights and shadows of a tropical sky.

The City of Palaces was now fully in sight,

and it was impossible not to be struck with the quiet beauty of the scenery. Before coming to it, the shores were uninteresting, and devoid of trees, which made the contrast more imposing. The banks rose before us, bold and richly clad with varied foliage; here and there handsome houses, seen jutting from the cover of the trees, were becoming more and more numerous; and Garden-reach presents a regular succession of magnificent villas and mansions, with parks and pleasure-grounds laid out in such a style that could not fail to give the traveller an idea of the owners' luxury and wealth.

Fort William now opens on the view, its green ramparts surmounted by numerous artillery, which, together with the regularity of its fortifications and the height and handsome appearance of its barracks, gives it an air of great importance, much aided by a very broad esplanade, beyond which is the city of Calcutta. The scene is very noble, and novel in its character, to any one seeing it for the first time.

The grand structures forming the residences of the official civil authorities, together with the palace of the Viceroy, or Governor-General, besides being in a style of architecture very different from what is to be seen in Europe, are most of them surpassing in splendour those seen there. Add to this the shipping and innumerable smaller vessels upon the water, the whole effect is wonderfully picturesque and striking.

But Calcutta and its environs are now so familiar and well known by numerous writers, that a further detailed account is unnecessary.

Having previously despatched a note to Alipore, the seat of Sir Charles Metcalfe, I received, in return, one from his Excellency's secretary, saying that Sir Charles had not arrived yet, but that apartments had been provided for me, that every attention should be paid on my arrival, and that a palanquin had been despatched to the nearest ghât on the river to take me there. Accordingly, at my last anchorage, I sent my servant forward, who found the palkee; and having had my last breakfast on board, and settled all things relating to the boat, &c., I started for Alipore, where I arrived in due course about tiffin, or lunch-time. Here I met some gentlemen at table, guests of Sir Charles, awaiting his arrival; and I had the pleasure of hearing all the news of passing events, and of the new arrivals from England. I was obliged to be content with the anticipated pleasure of meeting them and some very handsome young ladies, whom I had not yet seen, but who were expected to grace Government House on the first reception held there after his Excellency's arrival, and the usual evening party, which was to be held in the afternoon of a day appointed for the purpose.

I believe a great deal of our happiness consists in variety, or in passing from one scene to another. Thus, for instance, nothing could well be more different from the gay and pleasurable life I had led at Cawnpore than the dull monotony I was about to lead for some months on board a boat to Calcutta, and yet I felt pleasure in the latter, being aided by my books, shooting, fishing, and sketching, together with some exciting scenes on my way down the river. Those resources failed in a great measure to interest me, and when again brought into pleasing and enjoyable society, it felt, as it were, going from one extreme to another; but then it was also especially exhilarating and agreeable.

Some days after, Sir Charles Metcalfe arrived, and, as the Governor-General was still in the Upper Provinces, Sir Charles was to act for him in every capacity regarding the government of the Lower Provinces. There was soon after held a levée for all the officials and military officers either serving in garrison here or on leave, and, amongst the rest, I made my bow, and had a card sent me next day to attend an evening party, ending with a ball and supper. On the ·12th of December the time duly arrived, and we—that is, the Acting Governor-General, his suite, and guests—set off from Alipore, where we had previously a grand dinner, to Government House, a most splendid mansion. People who have never been in India can have no idea of the splendour and magnificence shown in buildings like this. The marble halls, the immense lofty rooms, and the ventilation so necessary to comfort in so warm a country, are here carried out to perfection. Then, when you arrive, how striking and delightful is the scene : the suites of native servants ranged tastefully around the rooms, arrayed in their snow-white muslin dresses, headed by their leaders, with silver badges of distinction; gentlemen and officers in full dress, and here and there, also, groups of English-women, some very handsome, the ladies elegantly attired in their newest ball-dress from London—all smiles and sweetness, waiting for their partners in the dance—form a sight, on entering, seldom or never seen in other parts of the world.

The Governor-General's band and the garrison band were in attendance, and in the first quadrille, Sir Charles Metcalfe, all good-humour and kindness, opened the ball. In due course, this was followed by waltzes and gallops. Did you need anything, a simple sign to a servant was enough to get it, and all went on happily—

> And bright
> The lamps shone o'er fair women and brave men;
> A thousand hearts beat happily; and when
> Music arose, with its voluptuous swell,
> Soft eyes looked love to eyes which spake again,
> And all went merry as a marriage bell.

At length supper was announced, when we handed our partners, and also took our places, to share the luxuries that surrounded us.

CHAPTER X.

1836—1842.

HAVING ascertained that the passenger-ships did not sail for Europe until the latter part of January or beginning of February, I secured a cabin on board one of Mr. Green's fine ships for England. As I had been living with Sir Charles Metcalfe for some time, I thought it but right to bid him farewell, and remove to the United Service Club, there to pass the remainder of my time, and amuse myself how I could, until the ship sailed.

On taking an affectionate leave of Sir Charles, he kindly expressed a hope of seeing me again, but I had not that pleasure. On his return to Europe, some time afterwards, his first-rate talents being well known, he was appointed Governor-General of Jamaica and the West Indies, then in a fearful state of disturbance, and which he quieted with his usual ability. He was most justly rewarded with a peerage, but, unfortunately for his country, he died soon after.

I found the United Service Club good, comfortable, and reasonable in its charges. It had also the appliances usually considered necessary to make it a desirable place to live in, particularly for a newly-arrived traveller from the interior of the country. While residing here, I occasionally visited some friends, and passed a few agreeable days, at Garden-reach, in a delightful residence. From thence I went to the Botanical Garden, which was well kept and in high order, and decidedly worth a visit; but I suppose it is now so well known that any description of it and of its manifold productions would be superfluous.

At the Chowringee theatre there were some pleasing actors, and, although they were not first-rate, still some of Colman's plays were creditably performed.

I had heard so much of the great pagoda of Juggurnaut, on the coast, that I was resolved to pay it a visit before leaving.

Juggurnaut is one of the numerous titles of the preserving deity, Vishnu, and signifies " supreme in the world." The temple is close to an ancient town upon the coast of Orissa, which is most desolate in appearance. It is, in fact, a succession of sandhills, without a particle of · vegetation, and presents to the beholder a melancholy sight. The town is not visible from the sea, but on the north side of the temple, which is seen at a great distance everywhere, there are a few bungalows, which form the European station, and these appear half buried in the sand. They, however, get the sea-breeze, which is a luxury in the hot season. The surf breaking on the shore is very great, and the massulah-boats, so useful on the Madras coast, are to be found here also.

The pagoda forms an excellent landmark to mariners on this coast. There is another pagoda, called "The Black Pagoda," which has a most uncouth appearance, and often causes mistakes to vessels approaching it. The Brahmins' tradition says that Juggurnaut is about four thousand years old. It is dedicated to Krishna* or Vishnu, Mahadhu or Siva, and Subhadra or Kalli.

The three figures are rough and ugly, being deficient of arms, and the faces are most absurd, both in form and in painting. The car in which these figures are drawn seems upwards of sixty

* There is a river so called, sacred to Krishna, dividing the Nizam's dominions from our territories south of that stream.

feet in height, daubed with paint. Vishnu, the preserving power in Hindoo mythology, is commonly represented as having a serpent in his grasp, extended over his head, and reaching to the ground; and the figure is trampling on the head of the reptile—a curious sort of corroboration of our primeval tradition. Siva, the destroying deity, is drawn with a serpent about his head, the hood of the reptile protruding above it. Kalli is the female personation of Siva, on whose altars thousands have been voluntary victims, until the great exertions of our Government suppressed these sacrifices, many years ago. Altogether, the whole scene is most grotesque, and extraordinary in a high degree; and it is revolting to think to what an extent infatuation can be carried in the minds of men of this faith. I was not sorry to quit the place and return to Calcutta.

Having received notice from my agent that the ship in which he had engaged a passage for me was, without fail, to sail on the 2nd of February, I went off to her on the evening before, accompanied by my servant and things. I found the vessel, which was a very fine one, surrounded with boats, in which were very many ladies and gentlemen, waiting their turn to be helped on board with their respective baggage. It was nearly dark before my turn came, when I scrambled on deck, and having got my effects to my cabin, left my servant and another man there to arrange it and my cot for sleeping, and went to the cuddy for refreshment, not having had any since breakfast. There I found a number of very young girls going home to be educated, sitting round a tea-urn and waiting to be served. The seat opposite it being the only one vacant, I sate down and had pretty good employment for nearly an hour before I was able to take anything for myself, and was pressed hard for tea—one saying, " Please, sir, my cup comes next; Lizzie has got a cup before her turn," and " Jenny has spilled her tea and scalded her mouth, and must wait her turn for the next "—and so on. However, I took it all patiently, and got something at last, luckily before the elders crowded in. On the juniors retiring, I was soon glad to retire myself.

In a few days, the passengers got things pretty right; we began to feel more comfortable, and were all told off to our respective places at the cuddy table. The captain appeared a pleasing and agreeable man, and the ship, which sailed on the morning of the 2nd, was well manned and served, so we all hoped for the best on our passage home.

At this time of the year there is generally a fair wind from the east, and fine weather, in a home direction, and we were fortunate enough to have both in perfection. On we went through the Bay of Bengal right merrily and happily. There were only two dissatisfied people among us, grumbling at everything. With this exception, notwithstanding our numbers, we got on very well together; the captain was especially good-natured, and very fond of children: he got up little dances for them on the quarter-deck. In this pastime I always joined, and hence I became a favourite with them. The coming heat told of our near approach to the line, which we crossed in a few days, being only inconvenienced by a heavy squall and some torrents of rain, which soaked some things exposed to it. Amongst the rest, my cabin was swamped, the window of which I had left open, it being a sultry night, and I was rather disagreeably awakened by a dash of sea entering and pouring a bath upon me, and wetting everything in the cabin.

I exerted myself to clear out the water, and on opening my boxes found them pretty dry. As they were all secured, I did not think, at the time, of a lower box, containing some books, my sketches and journals, and when I did, some days afterwards, found them utterly spoilt; the sketches quite a soft pulp : this was from a small quantity of water having remained in a corner of my cabin, where this box lay, and caused the mischief. We cannot at all times help these small accidents, so I thought it best to be reconciled to my lot, though at first I was very much vexed at it.

It is needless to enter into the usual every-day incidents that occurred on board during our passage home, which was accomplished in less than four months. We landed at Portsmouth, all well, and on my arrival in London, received orders to take charge of the depôt of the 63rd, my new regiment, at Chatham, in July, 1836.

This depôt required a good deal of attention to get into order. Drilling young recruits and looking after them was constantly required, and I remained at this work, with short intervals of leave, about two years. An order at last came to be ready to embark, in charge of a large body of troops, including the soldiers of my regiment, for the East, which in nowise displeased me, being heartily tired of home service.

We embarked in June, 1838, on board the

Mount-Stuart Elphinstone, Captain Jolly, for Burmah. The Tenasserim provinces of that empire had been recently ceded to us by the sovereign of that country, and it was there that the 63rd Regiment was stationed.

We had a fair average passage, and arrived off Moulmein, the chief town of the above provinces, in the latter end of the year. Here I found my very old friend and brother campaigner, Colonel Logan, in command of the 63rd Regiment, which he had in excellent order, and we were received by him with great kindness.

As the Burmese Government had shown every disposition to be hostile, we had in these districts a pretty strong force, consisting of the 62nd and 63rd British, and four regiments, regular and irregular, of the Indian service, with two batteries of European artillery, all under Brigade-General Hillier; a frigate, off the port, and two sloops of war, under Captain Kuper, Royal Navy; so we were prepared for any attack either by land or sea.

The Burmese appear a fine warlike people, their war-boats beautifully constructed, and are rowed by their crews with vigour and considerable skill.

As the Burmese outposts were in some force at the town of Martaban, opposite to us, about half a mile across the Tenasserim river, we had strong pickets posted at eligible points, on the look-out, and boats from our squadron, manned and armed, in readiness to meet any sudden attack that might be made upon us.

At this time we were at war with China, with whom the Burmese Government were in alliance.

Our forces, both naval and military, led an agreeable, I may say, jolly life, dining with each other, alternately, and ever on the most friendly terms. The climate we found healthy, and by no means so hot as the plains of India; but when the monsoon sets in, the rain pours down a continuous stream for months, so constant, that confinement in doors is a matter of course, and people must amuse themselves the best way they can. The houses, although built of wood, being raised from the ground two or three feet, on piles, and walled and thatched with matting, perfectly exclude wet, and are warm and comfortable. On the whole, we found this station much to be preferred before most places in India; here, as there, the finest scenery prevails, and the trees are of great size; the bamboo-tree, in particular, rises to a towering height: the top and branches, bending downwards in graceful and wavy folds, are beautiful in the extreme.   The religious houses, dedicated to Budh, are most picturesque buildings; their exquisitely formed spires, and pennants floating from them, in honour of this religion, are very striking to look upon.

Fires are of frequent occurrence amongst the native villages, from the inflammable nature of the houses, and the British troops are always employed to extinguish them, which is sometimes very hard work.

The Chinese war continued to prove favourable to our arms, which in all probability prevented the Emperor of Burmah from attacking us, and our time passed on pretty much as usual, as far as duty was concerned, and several years rolled over happily enough, the officers procuring leave for short periods, to visit the interior of the country, or on sporting excursions.

We all had Pegu ponies, which are admirable animals for racing, their speed, for their size, being wonderful. They afforded us much amusement, and some of our spare time was occupied in training them.

In the beginning of the year 1840 I got leave to accompany Drs. Woodford and Moreton, of the Indian service, on a tour up one of the rivers of this country, running towards Siam, from the seacoast, called the Attaran, which had not yet been explored by any European, the banks of which river were said to abound with curious animals and birds of great beauty.

We had two boats—one large one for our own accommodation, covered with a bamboo awning, and well fitted up with berths, tables, &c., the fore part being occupied by the boatmen; the other boat was a smaller one, for cooking, &c.

On the 3rd of March we left Moulmein, and proceeded for several days up the river with the tide, shooting many birds of handsome plumage on the way. Dr. Woodford was a naturalist, and on the evening of each day we landed, dined, and then commenced preparing our birds for stuffing.

On the morning of the 10th the scenery on the right bank of the river burst upon us with great magnificence—rocks, in Alpine beauty, running upwards three or four hundred feet, here and there studded with flowering shrubs, covered with red and white blossoms, and ever-greens of every size and colour, behind which the reflection of the sun appeared as a blaze of beauty. This enchanting scenery lasted the whole day—we stopped to admire it.

At another time, as evening closed, we saw a wide chasm in a rock, surrounded by festoons of creeping plants exactly like a Gothic window of the largest size; and at night we became impressed with the idea that a mighty range of grotesque buildings stretched out before us, while the river, lit up by the moon in silvery brightness, wound round the rock, which we called Cathedral Rock.

The next day we were again on our way, when we fell in with a set of gipsies, called here Careens, a wandering people. They have no fixed residence like their tribe in other places, living a sort of pastoral life, and looked contented and happy.

Shot some wild duck and moorfowl. Pea-cocks used now and then to show themselves, but the jungle on each side of the river was so thick that we could not get at them.

We were above the influence of the tide some sixty miles, and now it was seen how well the boatmen used their oars, pulling against the stream.

For the last two days we had much rain and stormy weather, after which it cleared up. We had now got up about eighty miles, and the climate was mild and invigorating.

We heard the lowing of the wild cow and buffalo, and saw several large hogs rooting in the ground, but they were too wary to let us come within shot. We had now sometimes to ascend rapids, and the boatmen used to drag us up them in shallow water. The stream ascended many small but charming islands, covered with wood and prickly shrubs and flowers, showing sometimes tiny, grassy plains. Indeed, the scenery was very charming.

On the 16th we came upon a party of Careens employed in charge of elephants, which are trained to guide teak timber down to the Tenasserim provinces. These elephants used to direct the timber in the river, so as to clear rocks and rapids; and it was most interesting to see with what skill the sagacious animals performed their task.

About the islands were numerous birds of the kingfisher species, various in size and colour, some white, dotted with black spots; others

were green, red, and blue; others, again, black,
streaked with red—these were the most beautiful. The fly-catcher was also in abundance,
generally of a dusky red, with long tail-feathers
and speckled throats.

The teak-tree in these forests grows to a
great size, and is well known to be the most
valuable timber in the East, no white ant
or other noxious reptile being able to prey
upon it.

Monkeys abound everywhere, of all kinds
and sizes, and occasionally the pretty white
monkey is seen with its tufted head. The
Careens told our servants that sometimes a
tribe of monkeys would emigrate to other parts
of the forest, and, in settling down on the part
they fixed upon, were often attacked by
others having previous possession, and that
a battle ensued, causing the death and injury
of many of them before the weaker party gave
way.

We thus proceeded, enjoying ourselves very
much, and, indeed, few excursions were attended
with the same satisfaction to all engaged. Thus
we went on until the morning of the 18th, when
we perceived, above a high bank, an open space
of some extent, on and about which we saw

peafowl and jungle-fowl in plenty. Here we proposed to remain a few days, when a very melancholy catastrophe brought our tour to an unexpected close.

In proceeding to give an account of the untimely death of one of our party, I cannot do better than give a "report" of the event, forwarded as soon afterwards as possible to my commanding officer, and which was published in the *Moulmein Chronicle*, of the 1st of April, 1840. It was to the following effect :—

"We have been permitted to publish the following letter from Captain Nevill, of Her Majesty's 63rd Regiment, addressed to Lieut.-Colonel Logan, commanding that regiment, reporting the particulars of the melancholy fate which befel Dr. Woodford, on the 18th of March last, as announced in our last number.

" The party consisted of Captain Nevill, Dr. Woodford, and Dr. Moreton, Honourable Company's service; the former attached to Her Majesty's 63rd Regiment.

" The latter gentleman appears to have had an almost miraculous escape from meeting with a similar fate; indeed, though the circumstance is not dwelt on in Captain Nevill's report, yet there is every reason to believe that Dr. Moreton's safety resulted from the firmness and intelligence displayed by that officer in these very trying circumstances.

" A more appalling situation cannot well be imagined than that in which Captain Nevill was placed, with one of his companions at the point of death and the other wandering in the jungle in the night, with the roars of tigers distinctly heard around him. To the happy thought of firing the jungle may Dr. Moreton's safety be ascribed, for we understand that that gentleman had gone so far from the river's bank as not to have heard the shots and shouts of Captain Nevill's party, while he distinctly heard the roars of tigers in different directions, and at one time found himself close to one of those animals. We have understood that the party had been previously warned by some natives to beware of the spot where they had put up for the evening, as it was known to be infested by tigers ; and, if this be the case, we would point out to all future explorers of the jungle the danger of deriding any advice they may receive from the natives of the country, who must be well acquainted with any dangers that exist, and whose advice is tendered to them with kindness, and friendly attention to their safety.

" The friends of Dr. Woodford must be grateful to Captain Nevill for his success in bringing his remains to town, there to be laid in consecrated ground. They were interred on the evening of the 28th ultimo, with military honours, attended by the brigadier in command of the troops, the Commissioner of the Provinces, and all the officers of the station, civil and military, by whom Dr. Woodford was much esteemed and respected."

REPORT.

" Right bank of the Attaran River, 19th of March, 1840, about one hundred miles from Moulmein by the course of the stream.

" SIR,

" It is in deep sorrow I have to announce to you the melancholy death of Dr. Woodford, in consequence of being struck down by a tiger while shooting in the teak forest here, the particulars of which are as follows :—

" I had just come in from fishing in the river close by where we dined, at about 6 p.m. on the 18th instant, when I saw Dr. Woodford stagger towards me. He said, 'Nevill, I have been

struck down by a tiger, and am a dead man.'
He then fell to the ground.

"I instantly had him removed into our boat,
and called for Dr. Moreton, who had just before
gone out.   On my administering some brandy-
and-water, Dr. Woodford somewhat recovered,
and stated that, seeing peafowl near him, he took
his gun and proceeded to them; he heard a roar
close to him, and, on turning his head, saw a tiger
in the act of springing upon him; he turned,
fired, and was rolled over by the tiger, but the
beast, being probably frightened by the fire,
dropped him and retired.

"Dr. Moreton not returning, I began to fear
that he had shared the fate of our comrade;
however, I assembled our boatmen and servants,
armed them with what I could, and proceeded
in quest of him, firing shots at intervals, to let
him know assistance was at hand, but without
avail, and I gave him up for lost.   I had seen
two tigers together from the river, and it was
this that made me hurry to my friends to tell
them of it.

"Seeing nothing further to be done, I set fire
to the jungle, remaining as near as I could to
it.   At half-past ten o'clock I heard a voice in
the distance calling for help, when, strange to

relate, there was Dr. Moreton, perched in a tree near the fire, whom we rescued quite uninjured. He stated that in walking out early in the evening, he had lost himself, to get out of the way of a tiger he saw close to him, and ascended the tree for safety. He hastened to render assistance to our companion, but at once pronounced his case to be hopeless, from the serious injury he had received, and towards the morning of the 19th he expired in great agony.

"I have the honour to be, Sir,

"Your very obedient Servant,

"(Signed) PERCY P. NEVILL,

"*Capt. H.M. 63rd Regt.*

"To LIEUT.-COLONEL LOGAN,

Commanding H.M. 63rd Regt.,
Moulmein.

"P.S. I send the remains of poor Dr. Woodford down to head-quarters in our light boat, and hope they will soon arrive. They are in straw, to protect them from the heat.

"4 p.m. 19th March."

The fate of poor Woodford cast a gloom over our mess for some days. He was a clever man and agreeable companion ; but, as all things in the course of time pass away, so at length did the recollection of this sad accident.

Nothing of any moment occurred out of the ordinary duties of military life during the rest of this year.

CHAPTER XI.

1841—1842.

IN 1841 the Chinese war was drawing to a successful close, and the hostile attitude of the Burmese Government visibly relaxed, so that we expected that the force would be reduced, if not for the most part withdrawn. Before this happened, three of the officers of the 63rd, namely, Major Pole, Lieutenant Haries, and myself, got leave to visit the interesting provinces of Mergui and Tavoy; and as the excursion to those places would be by water, we engaged a large square-rigged vessel, used on the coast and inland seas of this country. The major very kindly undertook to look after ourselves and our mess on board, and we were soon ready to sail, having all our stock of provision and wine on board.

Early in February we set sail on the splendid Tenasserim river, or rather, to a certain extent, branch of the sea, running towards Mergui, Tavoy, and Yea, the channel in some places

R

narrowing, and then expanding to large inland lakes, studded with islands, all grand,
picturesque, and imposing, well wooded, and
beautiful.

In a few days we made the town of Yea. The
scenery hereabouts is very charming, a very
pretty and extensive sandy bay stretching round
it ; and there are many wooded islands sprinkled
about.

The town of Yea exemplifies those de-
scriptions of beautiful scenery that we read
of, but are so seldom realized. There are
charming indented coves, covered with moss,
ivy, and flowers of various kinds, overhanging
the beautiful bay, and shaded at intervals by
the graceful waving bamboo-tree.

The houses and cottages in this sweet place
are built with great taste, and the inhabitants
look happy, their faces beaming with intelligence and tranquillity.

We thoroughly enjoyed ourselves, and walked
about the bay until the moon rose brightly,
throwing its halo around, and never in all my
travels did I see a spot of such surpassing
beauty.

Having remained a few days here, we proceeded to Mergui, sailing on a light blue sea,

clear and bright with the morning sun. On the 14th we arrived there, after passing a squally night, accompanied by thunder and lightning.

Mergui is a fine, bold, mountainous island. The town of the same name rises from the shore above you: it is a large place, and contains about twelve thousand inhabitants, all looking, as at Yea, contented and happy. The fish is here good and abundant, and we caught a flattish fish, which tasted much like our turbot.

A bold promontory rises on a small island close to the town, which is called Madame MacKane's Island, from a French admiral's wife, who lived for some years here, and, dying suddenly, was buried near her residence. A tomb, rising up conspicuously from the harbour, marks the spot.

There are missionaries of various creeds at Mergui, who visit the neighbouring islands, which we passed on our way, but as yet they do not appear very successful in their mission.

There was a detachment of our regiment here, under Captain Spier, a married man, with a family, who were all glad to see us, and hear the news. There was also a company of native Madras infantry, and a diplomatic friend, Captain Macleod, who had been Commissioner at the Court of his golden-footed Majesty, the Emperor of Burmah and of all the white elephants. Such was the style of the prince in this country.

We sailed on the 18th, passing some fine island scenery, and arrived at the ancient city of Tenasserim on the 20th. This town is now one vast ruin, with the remains of many magnificent temples, covered with creepers and shrubs of various kinds.

A coal-mine was discovered by some exploring party lately, which was worked, under charge of Lieutenant Hutchinson, of the Madras Artillery, aided by a small steam-engine, and yielded a good return of coal; and it was said that those provinces abounded in mines of tin and copper ore, with other minerals.

Travellers exploring this city ought to be cautious how they proceed, as there are the remains of old wells and watercourses, so grown over with verdure that it is hardly possible to make them out before you are upon them—many of which are of great depth.

We sailed from Tenasserim on the 24th, coasting along the shore, and sometimes obliged to anchor off small islands, to avoid the stormy weather that occasionally paid us a visit, and which is dangerous to such craft as we were sailing in; we therefore did not reach Tavoy until the end of the month.

Tavoy is a large province; the town nearly twice the size of Mergui, with thirty thousand inhabitants. The roads throughout are excellent, and the land so good and well cultivated, that the revenue gives a surplus, after all local expenses are paid. The people are remarkably civil, and well disposed towards us.

The markets are very good, and they have for sale, very cheap, the finest domestic fowls possible. The girls, and many married females, are handsome, and extremely well made — tall, graceful, and winning in their manner, their colour a light brownish yellow. Here were a detachment of European Madras Artillery, and a company of the 33rd Native Infantry; and here I again had the pleasure to meet my friend and old associate of the Attaran adventure, Dr. Moreton, in medical charge of the station.

The officers of the native troops had a tame toucan. This bird was nearly as large as a turkey, with a great beak, terminating in a point of nearly ten inches in length. It fed on pieces of uncooked meat, raised one at a time, and thrown some feet up, the toucan receiving it back with distended jaws, down its huge throat. When angry, it made a loud rattling hissing noise. It was a curious bird.

There is plenty of game of nearly all kinds in this fine country; and the long line of beautiful groves, dedicated to the Buddhist religion, with their quaint spiral buildings, containing several idols, some of great size, are peculiarly striking in effect.

Here we remained, enjoying ourselves, ten days; but as our term of leave was drawing towards a close, we put to sea, and sailed in the direction of Moulmein. On our way back we grounded on a sandbank, and were left so, high and dry, by the tide; in a few hours, however, the tide returned, and with the assistance of the boatmen, we were floated off without any injury, and proceeded with light winds on our way. We passed several of the pretty islands again, and made up our minds to pay a last visit to the charming province of Yea, which we reached on the 17th of March, and just in time to witness one of the grandest ceremonies to be met with at the far East. It was in honour of the dead.

When a priest (*Phoongee*) of the Buddhist

religion dies, he is embalmed; and if of a certain age and sanctity, more care and expense are taken in the doing so than if he were a crowned head. He is then put in a case filled with honey, and there he remains for several months, under a splendid sarcophagus, placed on a platform, close to the monastery or college he belongs to. The body is watched over by a select number of the priesthood of the deceased's class, night and day, without intermission, until the period arrives when it is to be consumed to ashes.

In the mean time, there is being made a gorgeous mausoleum of woodwork, beautifully carved and gilded, in which work all the most expert carvers and gilders are employed. This elaborate and lofty structure is executed voluntarily, without emolument, by those engaged. It is of a rectangular form, varying from ten to fourteen feet in length, eight in breadth, and fifty feet in height. Ascending from the base are open compartments; in these compartments are carved and gilded allegorical representations of the transmigrations the priest is supposed to be obliged to go through, at length ending in the soul's perfection, which then becomes fit for the presence of the Creator.

This I believe, from what I have read, to be the chief doctrine of the Buddhists.

I did not hear by what sign in the planets the priesthood are governed in selecting the proper time to consume the body of the deceased, but when they have decided that the time has arrived, it is announced to the people, who are prepared to attend the ceremonial.

When the day selected arrived, upwards of ten thousand people had assembled around the mausoleum, upon the top of which the sarcophagus had been placed.

The firing of this splendid piece of workmanship was to take place as the evening sun was about to sink below the horizon; and in the mean time the crowd appeared to enjoy the occasion with great glee, and amused themselves in various athletic games, such as wrestling, lifting heavy weights, and running foot-races; also in letting off fireworks. The women (and there were a number of unmarried damsels present) engaged in a sort of circular dance; they in no wise disguised their features, and seemed joyous and happy.

The wrestling parties did their best to throw each other, and some heavy falls took place, in which not one of the defeated party showed the least sign of rudeness or ill-temper; on the contrary, coming up to and shaking the victor cordially by the hand.

As evening came on, three handsomely-gilded cars arrived, in which were placed figures of celebrated warriors, as large as life, each holding diagonally a good-sized rocket. They were placed in a line about sixty yards from the mausoleum, and as the sun was setting the first rocket was pointed and fired, but missed the mark. The second was let off, but also missed, when a venerable man, in his yellow monastic dress, came forward, kneeled in prayer, then presented and fired the third rocket, which struck the mausoleum, and it was instantly in a blaze, ascending to the sarcophagus like lightning, which was soon in a dense flame of fire and smoke. This continued until the top fell in a heap of ashes: it was beautifully done. The people sent forth a continuous cheer, and then retired to their homes contented and happy.

And here it may be said that the people are justified in their partiality to their priesthood. They educate all classes; they advise and feed the poor; they are without prejudice towards others though differing in faith, and lead them-

selves, without exception, an excellent and
inoffensive life.

The Burmese people appear to be generally
extremely well-disposed and happy-minded, and
only want a good government to make them
a great nation.

On the 26th, we sailed, and made Amherst
on the 30th; in the evening of the next day,
we anchored off Moulmein, our head-quarters.

The latter end of this year Her Majesty's 62nd
Regiment was withdrawn from this station, also
the 14th Madras Native Infantry. Colonel Logan
was now the chief, and well worthy was he to
be so; he knew his duty right well, and used
to manœuvre the force under him with much
ability, showing us how fields were won. His
kindness and hospitality were proverbial; indeed
he truly was the right man in the right place.

We continued to get on, under such a man,
every way to be wished, until a rather sad
separation took place. It was towards the
latter end of July, 1842, that a sudden order
arrived to send a wing of our regiment across
the Bay of Bengal to Madras, from whence it
was to march to the ceded districts, where it
was rumoured some disturbances were likely
to take place.

The left wing was directed to go, and I was destined to take the command of it, and prepared accordingly. Early in August, the ship arrived that was to convey us to our destination and we embarked at once.

Accompanying one of my horses was a peacock, a very fine one, which voluntarily attached itself to this horse, and seemed quite unhappy when away from him. I inquired who owned it, but nobody seemed to know anything about it. On seeing this horse hoisted on board, the peacock flew. there also, and sailed off with us.

The moths and butterflies of Burmah are very large and beautiful, particularly the argus moth. I procured a good store of them for home.

We were five weeks on our passage, and landed in September at Madras, from whence we proceeded to the depôt established for the Queen's forces, where we rested for a few weeks, and then marched for the ceded districts.

Not long after we heard that the force in the Tenasserim provinces of Burmah was entirely broken up, and that the head-quarters and right wing of the 63rd Regiment were directed to join us.

Towards the close of 1842 we reached our destination, and happily without many casualties from sickness, although our route lay in a direction where that Indian scourge, cholera, was known to prevail. I never halted where I heard it was, but moved a few miles to the right or left out of the way; add to this precaution, we were favoured by cool weather.

CHAPTER XII.

1842—1848.

ON entering Bellary, the head-quarters of a large force stationed there, I was met by General Woulfe, commanding those districts, to whom I made my report, which seemed to give satisfaction, and I placed my men in the European barracks assigned me at this station.

The town of Bellary is surrounded by a strong fortification much on the native system. On a high rock, within some half-mile of the place, is another fort, washed at its base by a large tank or piece of water, at which thousands of people assemble to bathe and cleanse their garments.

In the upper fort was confined a nuwaib or native prince, formerly the sovereign of the ceded districts. The rock on which the upper fort stands is well known from its intense heat, as it reflects the sun's rays; and the plains around are amongst the hottest in this part of India.

We had plenty of duty; the force, consisting

of five native regiments, a portion of European artillery, and ourselves, were in the field every second day—this being the cool season, advantage was taken of it to manœuvre the troops. We were thus employed until towards the latter end of February, at which time the hot weather commenced.

Early in February a grand Mahomedan feast was to take place near the upper fort and around the rock on which it stands, at which all the believers of that religion, far or near, were to be present.

The day before this ceremony took place, I was waited on by the late highly-distinguished General Neil, who fell at Lucknow, then Deputy-Adjutant-General of the ceded districts, and presented with a *confidential* memorandum from the general, stating that I was to have all my men ready accoutred at nightfall on the following day; to have the gates of the fort closed, and no egress or entrance allowed during the festival; and to march out with two hundred men towards the fort road on a given signal: the rest of my men to keep constantly patrolling the streets of the town. Thus prepared, we continued in readiness to act if required.

At about 10 p.m. the uproar outside became

tremendous, when the blue rocket—my signal—was fired high in the air, and at nearly the same time the whole country appeared one blaze of light.

I sallied forth to the appointed place, where a multitude of men, many of them armed, worked up by excitement to a perfect frenzy, were ready to commit any act of violence. When they saw me a number of them rushed forward, when I ordered my captain* of light company to extend his men, but not to load without orders, nor use the bayonet fatally if possible.

On came the armed men, and down came the fixed bayonets of the Light Bobs. On the word to charge, the multitude gave way, but a few resolute men met and struck at us with their swords; however, the white faces and the bayonets made them turn and fly.

I halted on the ground, covered with fires, fireworks, and some arms, for more than an hour, but as there was no further assemblage, I marched back to quarters.

* The distinguished Lieutenant-Colonel Swyney, C.B., commanding the 63rd Regiment: killed at the battle of Inkerman.

The next day I received a note from the Deputy-Adjutant-General as follows :—

(Copy.)

"BELLARY, 29*th Feb.*, 1843.

" DEAR MAJOR,

" The General desires me to express to you his entire satisfaction at the manner you conducted your men last night, which proved most effectual without loss of life.

" The appearance of Her Majesty's 63rd on the scene was not expected, and the General did not wish to employ native troops.

" Believe me, dear Major,

" Faithfully yours,

(Signed) GEO. SMITH NEIL,
A.D.A.G.

" Major NEVILL,
" *Com. L.W. H.M. 63rd Regt.*
&c. &c.

In March it became very hot, and I began to think my long service of thirty-three years was beginning to tell upon me, as I was unable to

bear up against the heat of India. The head-
quarters and right wing of the regiment were on
the march to join us, and had unfortunately
suffered much from cholera.

They arrived in April, and their appearance
was most distressing; all the men looked un-
well. Three officers and a large number of
soldiers, some of the best we had, were carried
off by that awful disease, the cholera.

I had prepared an abundance of hot coffee,
and had served out to each man a glass of
brandy, and messes of nutritious curry were
ready prepared for them. For the officers there
was a good supper, and plenty of champagne,
and the looks of all were visibly improved in a
few days.

Having given over my charge of the left
wing, I obtained sick-leave to the Neilgherry
Hills, which I lost no time in availing myself
of, and there, by the influence of a cool and
pure air, soon was much better.

The appearance of those regions are much
like the mighty Himalayas, but on a
small scale. The inhabitants of them are
a distinct race from any other I ever saw,
are of a dusky yellow colour, and generally
small in stature. They live entirely amongst

s

themselves, and communicate with no one else. Their principal occupation appears to be to rear and keep large herds of black buffalo, whose milk is their principal food.

In attending divine service at St. Stephen's church, I observed near the altar, some lines recording the memory of my relative, Lady Rumbold, whose remains are interred here. The last time I saw this lady she was in her bloom of beauty, admired and loved by all who had the pleasure of knowing her.

When sufficiently recovered I rejoined my regiment, and served with it until the commencement of the hot season of 1844, when weakness and ill health again attacked me, and I became so depressed that I was advised to return to Europe. I therefore applied for leave home and retirement, which, having obtained, I hurried by post to the coast, and was lucky to find the good ship *Duke of Argyll* ready to sail for England, and a cabin vacant, which I immediately occupied. We sailed in a few days, and had a prosperous voyage to England, which we reached in August, without incident of any kind occurring worthy of notice.

My health on arriving in England was much

improved, but the winter season was too severe for my weakened frame, and a trip to the south of France was recommended. There I lived for some time, only to find out that the disease of all those who had served long in hot climates had got dominion over my constitution—that is, the liver complaint, which I felt sometimes very severe, and at length caused me, at the recommendation of a Medical Board, to retire from the army, on obtaining the brevet rank of Lieutenant-Colonel.

Having now for some time nothing to do, and my health gradually getting better, I purchased a commission in the Honourable Corps of Gentlemen-at-Arms.

My principal duties in this state corps were in attending Levees, Drawing-rooms, and Installations of the Orders of the Garter and the Bath, &c. Sometimes the rooms at St. James's Palace were so crowded with company, that it was no easy matter to dispose of them satisfactorily. Conceive something like six hundred people pressing together where there was hardly room for half that number.

It was an interesting sight, however, to behold all the influential and mighty of the land,

and the most beautiful women in the world, in their splendid attire, come to pay homage to our ever Gracious Queen.

The ambassadors' room was also full of attraction and novelty; and the throne-room, with the greatest of sovereigns present, surrounded by the great officers of state, had a most grand and imposing effect.

It occurred that, at one of the Drawing-rooms, my attention was drawn to the appearance of a magnificently-dressed Indian chief, who wore over his muslin trousers, knicker-bocker fashion, a pair of English top-boots. This looked most ludicrous, and what induced him to add the top-boots to his costume nobody could think.

On going up to him I recognised that it was Aza Mullah Khan, agent to the now notorious Rajah Nana Sahib, of Bithure, whom I formerly met there. He knew me at once, and I told him that no gentleman ever came to be presented in top-boots, and that he had better change them for his usual embroidered sandalled slippers. He instantly retired from Queen Anne's room and did so, returning quite in time for presentation.

In India, to wear leather of any kind on

state occasions, before a crowned head, would be looked upon as a great insult, and this gentleman knew it well enough.

In 1848 the Revolution in France broke out, and it was whispered it might be connected with Mr. Fergus O'Connor's chartist demonstration; thus it was necessary to be prepared for any outbreak that might occur. But we had few troops of any kind in England at that time, and the late Duke of Wellington advised that all public establishments should be armed and defended by those they belonged to; amongst the rest that the Palace of St. James's should be held by the Yeomen of the Guard and the Gentlemen-at-Arms. We accordingly received firearms, but found them too heavy for our drill, which was that of a dismounted troop of cavalry. Lord Combermere, on hearing this, most kindly lent us the spare carbines from his first regiment of Life Guards, with his regimental corporal major, to assist our drill. Lord Foley, our chief, made two of us military men sub-officers, and in a few months we became quite efficient.

The French Revolution, however, passed away, with the dethronement of the good King Louis-Philippe, by whom, in other days, I was presented with the Cross of the Legion of Honour, for my humble services on board his ship, *The Bengalie*, on her passage from India to Europe in 1831.

CONCLUSION.

The seas are quiet when the winds give o'er;
So, calm are we when passions are no more;
For then we know how vain it was to boast
Of fleeting things so certain to be lost.

Stronger by weakness wiser men become,
As they draw near to their eternal home :
Leaving the old, both worlds at once they view,
That stand upon the threshold of the new.

WALLER.

DO·what we may, time passes away, and we advance in life without thinking how fleeting it is—that those dear to us are gone, and that we ere long must follow them.

Since my recent retirement to Windsor, the full force of the above truth is often brought before me, amidst the sacred and beautiful service daily rendered in St. George's Chapel.

It was in the spring-time of this present year 1863, that I was so fortunate as to witness, in that gorgeous place of worship, a most brilliant and interesting ceremony, the marriage of

His Royal Highness the Prince of Wales with the Princess Alexandra of Denmark, on which great occasion the Royal Family of England attended, and all the illustrious and noble dignitaries of the land were present.

Great preparations had been made, and the admirable spectacle was ably arranged and carried out by Viscount Sydney, the Lord Chamberlain, so that nothing was wanted to add to its perfection.

There were three grand processions, each headed by the Queen's band.

First, the Royal Family, and then the illustrious and princely attendants of Her Majesty's household; then His Royal Highness the Bridegroom and his brilliant suite; next Her Royal Highness the Bride, marked by us all with surpassing interest.

The programme itself, pointing out all who were present and eminent by their princely and exalted rank, renders a detail unnecessary. Suffice it to say that the beauty and interest of the scene was charmingly done, and the most perfect order prevailed amongst the company through which the several grand processions passed. Not a hand was moved or a whisper heard throughout the entire ceremony.

My notice of the above memorable event, gentle reader, closes my little book and its many faults. To any who favour me by reading it I bid a kind farewell.

NOTES.

(*Copy.*)

CAMP, NARRINPOOR, INDIA.
Sept. 27, 1825.

SIR,

Last night we had a most severe storm of thunder, lightning, and rain, by which some of the men were injured, but not fatally, and five stand of arms destroyed and some baggage cattle.

Brevet-Captain Nevill's tent was entirely consumed, and all it contained, except himself. He was asleep inside at the time, and wholly uninjured. His escape appeared miraculous.

I have the honour to be, &c.,

(Signed) JOHN DALRYMPLE,
Major Commanding.

(*Copy.*)

From General Sir J. Burgoyne, Bart., G.C.B., Inspector-
General of Fortifications, &c.

War Office,
30*th March*, 1861.

My Dear Col. Nevill,

You indeed have every right to appeal
to me.

I have a very grateful remembrance of the
gallant services of the Officers of the Line, who
came forward in arduous times to act as
Assistant-Engineers at the Sieges in Spain,
when our Corps were so miserably deficient.

And amongst those gallant officers you were
one of the most distinguished.

Yours faithfully,

(Signed) J. F. BURGOYNE.

Lieut.-Col. P. Nevill.